"I need you to stay.

"I mean, I want you to stay," Ross corrected.

Jessica lifted her feathery brows over questioning eyes, but said nothing,

"Let me explain."

"I'm listening."

"We have a situation here—"

"We?"

"I have a situation. At least, the sheriff's department does."

"Yesterday's shooting?" Jessica asked.

He nodded. "We don't know what we're facing. There's the possibility what's happened to you is totally unrelated to other incidents in Swenson County."

"So if I leave tonight, I'm no longer your problem," she reasoned.

"I can't let you do that."

Her eyes widened with a hint of anger. "You can't stop me."

"Actually, that's not completely true."

"What are you going to do?" she insisted hotly. "Arrest me?"

"If I have to," he answered easily.

Dear Harlequin Intrigue Reader,

Take a very well-deserved break from Thanksgiving preparations and rejuvenate yourself with Harlequin Intrigue's tempting offerings this month!

To start off the festivities, Harper Allen brings you *Covert Cowboy*—the next riveting installment of COLORADO CONFIDENTIAL. Watch the sparks fly when a Native American secret agent teams up with the headstrong mother of his unborn child to catch a slippery criminal. Looking to live on the edge? Then enter the dark and somber HEARTSKEEP estate—with caution!—when Dani Sinclair brings you *The Second Sister*—the next book in her gothic trilogy.

The thrills don't stop there! *His Mysterious Ways* pairs a ruthless mercenary with a secretive seductress as they ward off evil forces. Don't miss this new series in Amanda Stevens's extraordinary QUANTUM MEN books. Join Mallory Kane for an action-packed story about a heroine who must turn to a tough-hearted FBI operative when she's targeted by a stalker in *Bodyguard/Husband*.

A homecoming unveils a deadly conspiracy in *Unmarked Man* by Darlene Scalera—the latest offering in our new theme promotion BACHELORS AT LARGE. And finally this month, 'tis the season for some spine-tingling suspense in *The Christmas Target* by Charlotte Douglas when a sexy cowboy cop must ride to the rescue as a twisted Santa sets his sights on a beautiful businesswoman.

So gather your loved ones all around and warm up by the fire with some steamy romantic suspense!

Enjoy,

Denise O'Sullivan
Senior Editor
Harlequin Intrigue

THE CHRISTMAS TARGET

CHARLOTTE DOUGLAS

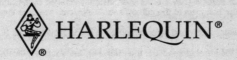

HARLEQUIN®

TORONTO • NEW YORK • LONDON
AMSTERDAM • PARIS • SYDNEY • HAMBURG
STOCKHOLM • ATHENS • TOKYO • MILAN • MADRID
PRAGUE • WARSAW • BUDAPEST • AUCKLAND

ISBN 0-373-22740-X

THE CHRISTMAS TARGET

Copyright © 2003 by Charlotte H. Douglas.

Visit us at www.eHarlequin.com

Printed in U.S.A.

ABOUT THE AUTHOR

The major passions of Charlotte Douglas's life are her husband—her high school sweetheart to whom she's been married for over three decades—and writing compelling stories. A national bestselling author, she enjoys filling her books with love of home and family, special places and happy endings. With their two cairn terriers, she and her husband live most of the year on Florida's central west coast, but spend the warmer months at their North Carolina mountaintop retreat.

No matter what time of year, readers can reach her at charlottedouglas1@juno.com, where she's always delighted to hear from them.

Books by Charlotte Douglas

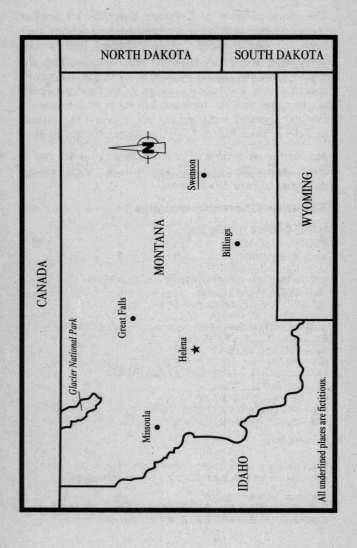

All underlined places are fictitious.

CAST OF CHARACTERS

Ross McGarrett—Heir to the Shooting Star Ranch and sheriff of Swenson County, Ross is plagued by unsolved crimes...and determined to keep beautiful Jessica safe.

Jessica Landon—Assigned to the Shooting Star as financial consultant, she's stalked by an unknown assailant.

Fiona McGarrett—Ross's grandmother has secrets of her own.

Courtney McGarrett—Ross's two-year-old daughter.

Chang Soo—Longtime chef at the Shooting Star Ranch.

Harry Chandler—Ross's friend and county judge.

Jack Randall—Ross's former father-in-law and neighbor with a boundary dispute. Is he as dangerous as he seems?

Carson Kingsley—He owns ranch adjacent to the Shooting Star.

Dixon Traxler—A client from Jessica's past who threatened her. Is he still a threat?

Prologue

The man kicked back in the deep leather chair in front of the fireplace, propped his aching feet on the ottoman and rubbed the twinge in his shoulder. He was getting older.

But not too old to complete his mission.

Besides, he assured himself, he didn't need brawn, only brains, to carry out his plans. Plus a ton of patience.

He had the brains. And he was a very patient man. He wouldn't rush things. First, he'd toy with his victims. He wanted them looking over their shoulders, flinching at shadows, suspicious of every little noise, fearful of every stranger, wondering what the hell was happening to them and knowing they couldn't do a damn thing about it. If they died suddenly, without fear, he'd miss half the fun.

Most of all, he wanted them to suffer for the trouble they'd caused. Only then would he remove them permanently from the face of the earth so they couldn't create any more.

Satisfied that his cause was right and just, he picked up the glass from the table beside his chair, swirled the ice in the amber liquid and downed the rest of his drink. He could afford time to relax. Everything was in place. All was ready.

Death would only have to cool his heels a little longer before claiming his own.

Chapter One

Santa with a shotgun?

Jessica Landon peered through the frost-rimmed glass door at the plump, red-suited figure in line at the teller window. None of the other customers paid any attention either to his costume or his weapon. Did everyone in Montana carry a gun?

Welcome to the Wild West.

The thought made her grimace. With a sigh of resignation, she tugged open the door at the First Bank of Swenson, fought the opposing force of the blustery December north wind and hurried into the lobby. Cold numbed her fingers in too-thin gloves, wet snow sifted down her neck beneath the stylish collar of her lightweight cashmere coat and icy slush soaked her feet, exposed to the elements by elegant but now-ruined high-heeled shoes. She wasn't accustomed to dressing for winter weather and, obviously, hadn't got it right.

Welcome heat greeted her, but not the familiar moist, tropical atmosphere of her native Miami. The dry, fusty air of a central system, apparently operating at its maximum potential, seared her lungs and dried her skin. Longing for the humid warmth of Florida sunshine, she crossed the lobby toward a desk marked Information, where a bank employee was conferring with an elderly lady.

"Excuse me," Jessica said, and shot a smile of apology at the older woman.

"Can I help you?" the bank employee asked.

"I'm here to see John Hayes," Jessica said.

"If you'll have a seat," the employee answered in a pleasant but distracted tone, "he'll be with you shortly."

Jessica settled in a chair a few feet away, unbuttoned her coat and refrained from fanning her cheeks in the unnatural heat. Ever since her boss, Max Rinehart, had escorted her aboard her flight at Miami International, she'd been either too hot or too cold.

Thinking of Max, probably sunning himself and sipping a tall, cool drink beside the free-form swimming pool of his Biscayne Bay home at this very minute, she uttered a silent curse.

He'd given her no choice in accepting this assignment. "You're the best consultant I've got," he'd insisted, "and our client demanded the best."

"*You're* the best, Max. You should be flying to Montana in the dead of winter, not me."

Max had grinned, flashing his amiable puppy-dog look that hid a savvy business mind. Brilliant sunlight streaming through the glass wall of his twelfth-story office glinted off his bald head, the wristband of his Rolex and the fourteen-carat gold buttons of his navy-blue blazer, tailor-made for his dumpling body.

"You know I can't go," he explained with an apologetic look. "The Christmas holidays are approaching. All the grandchildren and their pals from college will be descending on me."

"What better reason to get out of town?" Jessica asked in a dry tone, but she knew how much Max doted on his grandchildren and that he wouldn't miss spending their vacation time with them.

He spread his hands as if to accent his helplessness in the situation. "With their grandmother dead, God rest her soul, they need someone here to keep them in check."

"So you're sending me to the boonies while you ride herd on the party animals? Thanks a bunch."

"Jessikins—" He rose from his desk and came to her, encircling her in a fatherly hug. "You've never made a secret of the fact that you hate Christmas and everything about it. I'm doing you a favor, giving you a challenging assignment to take your mind off your least favorite time of year."

She couldn't argue with him about disliking the holidays. From the time she was six until she was eighteen, she had spent every Christmas vacation alone in the cold impersonal dormitory of the New England boarding school where her parents had shunted her after their nasty divorce. As a result, she'd hated the Yuletide season and cold weather ever since.

"You're all heart," she said grumpily, but in spite of her irritation at the impending job, she could never stay angry with lovable Max. With her parents re-married—her mother was on her fourth husband, her father, his third wife—and flitting from one European playground to the next, Max was the closest thing to family she had. She returned his hug and offered him a teasing challenge. "I could forget Christmas even better during a few weeks on the beach at St. Thomas."

"You bring back your report by January sixth, and I'll give you the rest of the month in the islands as a bonus," he had promised.

Remembering, she sighed and considered removing her coat in the bank's heat. January couldn't arrive fast enough—if she didn't either freeze or cook to death before then.

The information officer launched into an explanation of social security direct deposit for the fragile old lady. Jessica shifted in her chair and glanced around the lobby. Except for the heavy clothing that bundled the customers against Montana's bitterly cold climate, the bank, with its contemporary decor in fashionable neutral tones and its jungle of potted tropical plants, could have been in Miami.

Seven customers, including the gun-toting Santa, waited in two teller lines. At a table near the entrance, a tall, rugged cowboy stood with his back to her, filling out what looked like a deposit slip. His attire, including a suede, sheepskin-lined jacket, a battered Stetson pushed back off his forehead, butt-hugging jeans and tooled leather boots, would definitely draw a few stares in Miami. Unlike the Santa, however, the cowboy didn't appear to be carrying a gun.

Jessica pulled her gaze from his long, lanky legs. Since the cowboy was apparently unarmed, maybe the West wasn't as wild as she'd imagined. Its famous mystique was undoubtedly a myth. Take the cowboy, for instance. As seductively attractive as he appeared from behind, he was probably missing teeth, reeked of horse sweat and cow hides and had breath as foul as her mood right now.

Her temper was rising because she didn't like waiting. She kept herself on a regimented schedule and could never understand why others didn't do the same. Efficiency was good for business.

She glanced toward the door of a private office across the lobby where a brass plaque read, John F. Hayes. Hayes was the bank manager Max had told her to contact, but the employee at the information desk hadn't informed him Jessica was waiting. She decided to take matters into her own hands and knock on Hayes's door.

Ignoring the cowboy's attractive denim-clad tush, Jessica conducted a mental review of Max's instructions as she pushed to her soggy feet and crossed the room toward Hayes's office. Her ability to concentrate on work to the exclusion of all else—that and her MBA from the Wharton School of Business—contributed to her success as a top-notch financial consultant and troubleshooter. Oblivious to everything but her assignment, she ran through a mental list of the questions she'd prepared for John Hayes.

Suddenly a bone-jarring jolt struck her and yanked her off her feet.

She yelped in surprise as strong arms surrounded her and jerked her against a chest as solid as case-hardened steel. The concurrent deafening blast of a shotgun and the cascading crash of the bank's front window drowned her cry. She struggled against the grip of the cowboy she'd noted earlier—until she spotted the Santa from the teller line, pointing the double barrels of his shotgun directly at her.

"I said nobody move," he shouted with an angry growl. "Don't you understand English?"

Jessica had been so deep in thought, she'd heard nothing the Santa had said until now. She froze in the cowboy's embrace—except for a quick flick of her eyes that took in the rest of the now-silent lobby. The customers stood ashen-faced, hands raised, with the panicked expressions of wild nocturnal animals caught in a sudden beam of light.

The snarling Santa hadn't been waiting in line for a legitimate transaction. His fluffy white beard and bushy eyebrows were a disguise. Beady yellow-brown eyes, like those of a cobra prepared to strike, glared at her. Jessica shivered as his cold stare bored into her. He'd shot out the window without hesitation and looked ready—even eager—to shoot again. The man was either totally reckless or out of his mind.

Or both.

Jessica swallowed hard against the terror rising in her throat and prayed silently that no one would try to be a hero. The crazed Saint Nicholas looked capable of blowing them all away without a qualm.

Behind the counter, a terrified young female teller was stuffing packets of bills into a bag as fast as her shaking hands would allow. Even under duress, Jessica's efficient and encyclopedic brain fed her information, reminding her that bank tellers were trained to hand over their money without resistance—and to insert a stack of bills with a dye pack that would explode once the robbers left the bank. She recalled that small-town banks were considered soft targets for thieves, with buildings that were less secure and escape routes that were more accessible and less likely to be heavily patrolled by law enforcement.

For an instant, Jessica, locked in the iron grasp of the cowboy's arms, wondered if the man who held her was the robber's accomplice and had grabbed her as a hostage. Then she noted the path the shotgun pellets had taken to the outside window and realized with a shock that the cowboy had probably saved her life. Lost in her mental review of her upcoming interview, she hadn't heard the robber's first warning to remain still, and he'd opened fire on her. Only the swift intervention of her rescuer, who had jerked her out of the buckshot's path, had saved her from being blasted to kingdom come, just like the bank's front window.

Her knees buckled at the could-have-been, and if the cowboy hadn't held her, she would have collapsed onto the desert-toned carpet.

"Steady." His low voice, rich and smooth as cubano espresso, filled her left ear. "Stay calm."

"Shut up," the pseudo-Santa yelled, "or I'll shoot you both."

Jessica dragged in a deep breath of the chilly air pouring through the shattered window, and with it, the tantalizing fragrance of leather, saddle soap, open spaces and the unmistakable provocative male scent emanating from her rescuer. He had molded his body against her back and buttocks with an intimacy usually reserved for lovers, and his heat seeped through the triple layers of her coat, suit and lingerie. His contact reassured and, at the same time, flustered her, but she didn't have long to dwell on the contradiction.

"Hurry up!" the robber screamed at the young teller. At the strain in his voice and the knowledge that he'd already shot to kill once, Jessica shuddered. Everyone in the room faced imminent danger.

The distraught teller shoved the last of the bills into the bag and flung it atop the counter.

The biting north wind carried the wail of an approaching siren through the demolished window. Someone must have triggered the silent alarm, Jessica thought. Hearing the siren, Santa grabbed the money-filled sack and swung it over his shoulder.

And laying his finger aside of his nose... Jessica choked back a hysterical giggle as the line from the traditional Christmas poem popped into her head.

With no chimney for his escape, Santa backed toward the front of the lobby. Swinging his shotgun in an arc that covered every person in the room, he warned, "You follow me, you're dead meat."

He lifted a dirty black boot over the low sill, stepped out onto the shards of glass that covered the sidewalk and disappeared at a trot down the practically deserted main street of Swenson.

Jessica sagged in relief against the stranger who held her, and chaos erupted in the lobby with everyone talking at once. A sheriff's car, blue emergency lights flashing, sped past the window in the direction the robber had taken.

The cowboy who'd rescued her grabbed her shoulders and swiveled her to face him. He was so tall, she found herself confronting the broad expanse of his chest.

"What's the matter with you?" Anger tainted the rich smoothness of his voice. "Are you deaf? Or just suicidal?"

Before she could reply, he turned from her and shouted across the lobby, "Nobody move or touch anything until I give the okay."

Still stinging from his rebuke, Jessica felt a flush of embarrassment mixed with irritation rising to her cheeks. Prepared to explain her behavior, she lifted her gaze from the open collar of his denim shirt to the man's face. Her excuse died on her lips, and her knees threatened to go weak again.

The cowboy mystique was alive and well in Swenson, Montana.

Gazing down from a lofty height of well over six foot four with a body as big and sturdy as a Humvee and eyes as deep brown as the mineral-stained waters of the Everglades, the intriguing man took her breath away. His face was too rugged to call handsome with its square jaw and high cheekbones, but attractive enough to make her pulse stutter. At the corners of his eyes and mouth, fine laugh lines crinkled skin as warm and golden as South Beach sands, and his wide, appealing mouth and strong chin had a determined set.

What was the matter with her?

She was gawking at her rescuer like a moonstruck teenager, expecting to hear the opening strains from *The Magnificent Seven* any second. Her close brush with death had addled her brain.

Hands that felt strong enough to snap her in two shook her gently, and his eyes filled with alarm. "Hell's bells, lady, don't faint on me."

His plea broke the spell, and she shook off his grasp. "I've never fainted in my life," she insisted with righteous indignation.

"There's always a first time."

Before she could protest further, he scooped her into his arms.

"Put me down. I'm perfectly capable of walking."

"No, you're not. And you're in no position to be giving orders."

Surprise took her breath away, stifling any more protests. He carried her across the lobby into Hayes's empty office and deposited her on a sofa.

"I'm okay—" She struggled to rise, but he pushed her back onto the sofa with a firm hand.

"Stay put." His tone left no room for argument. He pivoted on his heel and headed toward the lobby.

"Wait!"

He turned at her call, and she was struck again by the man's magnetic charm. Accustomed to addressing conference rooms filled with international captains of industry, Jessica found herself suddenly tongue-tied in front of one incredibly attractive cowboy.

His wide mouth lifted in a slow, bone-melting grin, and amusement lit his eyes at her extended silence. "Well?"

"I… Thank you. You saved my life."

"Just doing my job." With a look that made her stomach flip-flop, he touched his fingers to the brim of his hat and stepped out the door.

Jessica propped herself on her elbows and watched him stride into the lobby, where the other customers and tellers had gathered. As her heartbeat returned to normal after revving at the stranger's sexy smile, her previous irritation at her current assignment rose to new heights. She hadn't been in Montana more than a few hours, and already she'd been shot at and man-handled. Max would have to cough up more than three weeks in St. Thomas to compensate for this.

She struggled upright, swung her feet to the floor and started to stand, but her knees wouldn't coop-erate. More shaken by her close brush with death than she cared to admit, she collapsed onto the sofa with a soft grunt.

She was where she'd intended to be, in John Hayes's office. She might as well wait.

Ross McGarrett left the woman in John Hayes's office and returned to the lobby. He was a man slow to anger, but at this moment he felt like Mount St. Helens ready to blow. The robber had not only come within a hairbreadth of killing a young woman, he had stolen hardworking people's money and scared a sweet old lady half to death.

Holding his temper in check, Ross waded into the midst of the frightened group in the bank's lobby and strode straight to the information desk where Miss Minnie Perkins was trembling like a leaf in a gale-force wind.

With the bank filled with people, he'd decided against using the gun in the holster at the small of his back to confront the fake Santa. Better to let the robber get away than to have someone killed. His decision, he realized, had been the right one when the man proved so trigger-happy. Ross's next instinct had been to follow the robber into the street. Then Josh Greenlea, the deputy on duty, had roared by in hot pursuit in his cruiser. With Josh on the felon's tail, Ross had decided to remain with the rattled customers and secure the crime scene until the technicians arrived.

Kneeling on one knee by the information desk, Ross grasped the old woman's cold hands. "You okay, Miss Minnie?"

All the color had drained from her weathered face. "I need my pills."

Ross opened her oversize handbag and dug out the bottle of nitroglycerin from among the jumble of wadded Kleenex and grocery coupons. He popped the cap and dumped one pill into her shaking hand, then thought better of that and gripped it between his fingers. "Open wide and lift your tongue."

Like a baby bird, Minnie did as he asked, and he tucked the pill beneath her tongue. "Want someone to drive you to the hospital?"

She shook her head. "I'll be fine now."

Renewed anger at the robber surged through Ross. If he lived to be a thousand, he'd never understand people who felt that laws didn't apply to them. As a young boy, Ross had been taught by his grandfather that law was the glue that held society together, and Ross's reverence for the law had eventually led to his election as sheriff of Swenson County. He took his sworn duty seriously.

And he took the breaking of the law within the county's borders personally.

Especially personal had been the murder of his wife, Kathy, last year....

With an effort, he shoved aside that pain and the unsolved mystery. One crime at a time, he reminded himself and moved swiftly through the lobby, speaking to each witness, consoling the distraught customers and easing them away from any possible forensic evidence.

The entire time, however, he found himself glancing into John Hayes's office, unable to keep his eyes off the beautiful stranger who'd come so close to perishing from the shotgun's blast. The floral fragrance of her shampoo, something tropical and exotic, still clung where his chin had brushed her sleek auburn hair when he'd yanked her from harm's way. Her provocative scent stirred feelings he didn't have time to deal with now.

Concentrating on the business at hand, he realized the attractive woman in Hayes's office had been one of two strangers in the bank that morning. The robber had been the other. His shot at her could have been a ploy intended to terrorize the others into submission. The probability that this petite and elegant woman was Santa's accomplice was a stretch, but Ross had to check out every angle.

"Everybody stay put till the Crime Scene Unit arrives," he warned the others after a call to dispatch, who assured him the CSU was en route.

Then he returned to Hayes's office.

At his approach, the woman leaped to her feet, all five foot three of her. She had seemed such a tiny submissive thing in his arms, but now she appeared ready to take on a wild grizzly five times her size. Her stylishly short coat and skirt revealed long, slender legs, and as he'd held her, he had registered the pleasant fact that she was deliciously rounded in all the right places. Her spunk as well as her appearance impressed him. No, spunk suggested too much heat. In spite of having come within inches of losing her life, the woman appeared cool and composed. Glacial was a better term.

"I'm Sheriff—"

"Where's John Hayes?" she asked abruptly.

Ross shrugged. "Probably taking a late lunch, but he'll be back soon if he's heard the news. Mind if I ask what you're doing here?"

She cocked her head and observed him with defiant blue eyes, dark and deep as a mountain lake. "You said 'sheriff.' Am I under arrest?"

"Should you be?"

"I may be crazy for coming here and for not hearing the robber's warning," she said in a rueful tone, "but I haven't done anything illegal."

"I'll need your name and address."

She slid the tiny strap of a fine leather handbag off her shoulder, snapped open the gold clasp and removed a business card. "Everything you need to know is right there."

With interest, he scanned the card, printed on heavy, expensive stock. She was Jessica Landon with Rinehart and Associates, Financial Consultants, out of Miami. The card appeared authentic, but anyone with a computer and the right paper could print one. "You're a long way from home."

Comprehension appeared to dawn suddenly in her eyes. "You don't think I had anything to do with—"

"Sheriff." John Hayes, the bank's manager, stepped into the office.

"You expecting this lady?" Ross asked. "Ms. Landon from Miami?"

John nodded. "We have an appointment." He turned to Jessica. "Sorry, but I'll have to postpone our meeting. Have you had lunch?"

The woman looked ready to protest the delay, then seemed to think better of it. "Is there a restaurant nearby?"

Ross nodded toward the opposite side of the street. "The café has great coffee. Good pies, too."

"I'm free to go?"

Ross nodded again, irrationally wishing for an excuse to keep her around until his sense of duty kicked in.

"Come back in an hour," John suggested with a glance at Ross. "I imagine the sheriff will be through by then."

"That should do it," Ross agreed, hoping the CSU would arrive promptly.

Jessica Landon straightened her shoulders, lifted

her chin and strode out of the office and the bank as coolly as if someone almost killed her every day.

TWO HOURS LATER, Jessica sat in the booth at the front of the café watching the controlled pandemonium at the bank across the street. Except for three rugged cowboy types, their weathered faces making their ages impossible to guess, one at the booth beside hers, the others at the counter, the restaurant was empty.

During her vigil, she'd watched the arrival of the Crime Scene Unit van, the departure of the customers, the removal of the glass from the front walk and the covering of the window with plywood. Throughout all the activity, the tall, handsome sheriff had been a constant presence, supervising, observing, instructing, and obviously completely in charge.

What struck Jessica most about the man, besides his distinctive good looks, was his apparent calm throughout the chaos. Nothing seemed to rattle him as he moved smoothly from task to task, person to person. He took the term *laid-back* to a whole new level. She could understand why the people of Swenson had elected him. He was without a doubt a good man to have around in a crisis. She just hoped he handled things quickly so she could meet with Hayes and get out of Dodge—or Swenson, as the case may be.

"Change your mind, hon?" The waitress with a name tag identifying her as Madge reappeared at her

elbow, shoved the mint she'd been sucking into the
pouch of her cheek and refilled Jessica's cup. "Want
to order now?"

Jessica had been nursing several mugs of decaf
while she waited for Hayes to become available, obviously longer than he'd anticipated. At first, her
close call had robbed her of her appetite, but she
hadn't eaten since breakfast, and at three in the afternoon, hunger made her empty stomach ache.

"I'll try some pie. The sheriff recommended it."

The middle-aged waitress grinned and winked, ex-
posing a lid caked with blue eye shadow. "You a
friend of the sheriff?"

"We met at the bank." How else could Jessica
describe her intimate encounter with the man who
had saved her life and set her senses tingling?

Madge made a clucking sound with her tongue.
"What a hunk. He can park his boots under my bunk
any day."

The bedroom image made Jessica flush with heat
in the already stuffy room, but she wasn't about to
discuss one stranger's attributes with another. "What
kind of pie do you have?"

Madge rattled off an impressive list, and Jessica
selected chocolate cream. In moments, the waitress
placed a huge wedge of pie topped with several
inches of meringue in front of her and nodded toward
the window. "Looks like they caught the crook."

Another cruiser had pulled up with a man in the
back seat, apparently handcuffed, judging from his

posture. The Santa suit was gone, but even from across the street, Jessica could recognize those cold, deadly eyes. The sheriff climbed into the passenger seat of the car, the deputy drove away and the Crime Scene Unit van followed.

Within minutes, an Open sign appeared on the bank's front door. Deserting her hardly touched pie, Jessica grabbed her coat, paid her bill and headed across the street.

ANOTHER HOUR LATER, Jessica left the bank in an even fouler mood than when she'd first arrived. In spite of what Max had hinted, she'd hoped this assignment would be quick, a day or two at most auditing accounts, perusing records and then writing up her assessment of the ranch's viability in the dubious comfort of her spartan hotel room.

Max and Hayes had made other plans.

All the paperwork she needed to complete her assignment was in the office of the Shooting Star Ranch, thirty-five miles outside of town. And Hayes had insisted that the trustees wanted a thorough inspection of the ranch, acreage, stock and buildings.

"The family's invited you to be their guest while you work," Hayes had said. "That way you won't have that long commute back and forth to the hotel and restaurants every day. The less you're on the road this time of year, the better. Driving can be treacherous."

"Then I should see you in a few days," Jessica said.

Hayes looked surprised. "Oh, I doubt that. You should take your time, observe for yourself the assets of the ranch and how it works. Plus you have over a decade's worth of accounts to evaluate. The trust insists on a complete evaluation of the property's productivity. Only when the trustees are satisfied that all is as it should be will ownership be transferred."

"Rinehart and Associates are never anything but thorough," Jessica said, wishing in this instance it wasn't so. She'd never been so homesick for Miami.

"Of course," Hayes said soothingly. "That's why the trustees selected you."

Climbing into her rental car with wet snowflakes plastering her cheeks, Jessica wished the trustees had picked another firm. She faced a thirty-five-mile drive in unfamiliar territory in increasing snow. Blessing the fact that her vehicle had snow tires, she pulled away from the curb, eased down the main street and took the turn Hayes had instructed.

Thirty-five miles south on this road; hang a right at the Shooting Star gate. Seemed simple enough.

Within minutes she was in deserted countryside where snow drifted against fences and turned rocky outcroppings and buttes into gigantic gnomes hovering in the cold. Working at maximum, the wipers barely kept the windshield clear enough for her to see the road ahead of her. The defroster on the rear window was minimally efficient. As much as she disliked the thought of being a houseguest among strangers, Jessica had to admit that not having to drive this far at least twice a day in this weather would be a relief. Not a single car had passed her coming from the opposite direction. The only vehicle she'd seen on the road was far behind her, headlights glaring and gaining fast. She guessed most of the natives had better sense than to risk driving in these conditions and cursed her own impatience. If she'd waited until morning, the snow might have ended.

The car behind her was closing in on her bumper. Only a fool would drive so recklessly on these icy roads, she thought. The dark pickup loomed large in her rearview mirror.

The truck swerved into the other lane, pulled alongside as if to pass, then slowed, keeping pace with her speed. She wondered if the driver was trying to signal her with some sort of message or warning, but she couldn't see through the dark-tinted glass of the pickup's passenger window.

She slowed so he could pass, but the truck beside her slowed, too.

Without warning and catching her totally off guard, the other vehicle lurched to the right and slammed into the side of her much smaller sedan.

Jessica fought the wheel to keep her car on the pavement. Luck, not skill, kept it from spinning into a skid, and she sighed with relief as she regained control.

The truck, however, remained alongside her. With

what seemed like predetermined intent, it smashed into the side of her car again.

In horrified disbelief, Jessica felt the sedan leave the road, airborne. With a sickening crunch of glass and metal, it plowed into a snowbank.

The world turned briefly white when her airbag deployed, and her body slammed painfully against the restraints of her seat belt.

Everything went black.

Chapter Two

Jessica, head throbbing, muscles stiff with cold, slowly regained consciousness. Moving gingerly, she tested her arms and legs. Nothing felt broken. She ran cold-numbed fingers over her body. No sign of bleeding or other injury. She was only bruised.

And freezing to death.

To her great relief, she discovered her door would open, and she climbed from the car. The sight that greeted her drove all further relief from her thoughts. The sedan had soared across a ditch and crashed into a wall of earth on the other side. Even if the car was drivable, she'd need a tow truck to extract it from its current resting place.

She scanned the area, searching, with mixed emotions, for the vehicle that had hit her. She needed someone to save her from the cold, but the driver of the pickup definitely hadn't had her welfare in mind. She should be glad he hadn't returned to finish her off. Maybe he figured she'd perished in the crash, and if she hadn't, the cold would kill her.

She didn't want to believe someone had run her off the road on purpose, but the person who caused the accident hadn't stopped to assist. A glance at her watch indicated at least fifteen minutes had passed since the collision. Her assailant was long gone.

The storm was intensifying, and if she didn't get help soon, she'd die from hypothermia. She tried her cell phone, but Hayes had already warned her it would be unreliable in this part of the country where relay towers were scarce. She was disappointed but not surprised when she couldn't receive roaming service.

Recalling vaguely hearing or reading something about staying with the car if stranded in a snowstorm—whoever would have thought a Miami resident would need that bit of info?—she started to climb back into the vehicle.

And smelled gasoline.

The tank must have ruptured. The ominous liquid was dripping from beneath the chassis and puddling in the ditch. Afraid to risk the danger of remaining in a potential fireball, she figured she should at least attempt to retrieve her luggage. Donning extra layers of clothing—even clothing woefully unsuitable for southeastern Montana's cruel winter climate—might be her only chance for survival.

The car had landed at an angle, and she had to struggle to drag her luggage from the trunk that rested shoulder-high. She carried her bag to the side of the road and hoped someone would pass and give her a lift.

If they could see her in the blowing snow.

Her head pounded, her bruised knees and shoulders ached, and she swore that Max was going to owe her big-time.

If she lived to collect.

She was on her knees, rummaging through her open case for additional clothing, when the howling wind carried the sound of an engine, approaching from the direction of town. Grabbing a red silk dress, Jessica raced to the center of the road and brandished the garment like a flag.

The car appeared suddenly out of the driving snow, almost on top of her. Jessica dived for the side of the road. The driver slammed on brakes, going into a skid that would have landed the SUV next to her car in the ditch without some first-class maneuvers on the part of the driver.

Jessica pushed to her feet and brushed snow from her ruined stockings.

The SUV's door opened. A massive man exited the car and descended on her like a charging bull.

"Hell's bells, lady! You got a death wish?" It was the sheriff from Swenson. Even hopping mad, he was the sweetest sight she'd ever seen. "You could have been hit, standing in the middle of the road like that!"

"I've already been hit," Jessica said hotly. "And if I hadn't been in the middle of the road, you wouldn't have seen me, and I would have frozen to death in this godforsaken wilderness.''

She doubted he understood a word she'd said, since her teeth were chattering so hard, her speech was almost incomprehensible.

He must have comprehended enough, though, because his anger seemed to leave him, like the air from a deflating balloon. ''Are you hurt?''

''Luckily,'' she managed to utter through her chattering teeth, ''not as badly as my car.''

She nodded toward the ditch, and the sheriff followed her gaze.

''Aw, sh—'' He bit off the curse, then turned and loped back to his car. He returned seconds later with a blanket, and without giving Jessica time to react, he'd wrapped her tightly, lifted her in his arms and settled her on the front seat of the deliciously warm SUV, his official car from the looks of the radio and shotgun mounted on the dash.

Before she could say a word, he returned to the roadside and made a quick inspection of the wrecked sedan. After gathering her luggage from the shoulder, he placed it in the back of the SUV and climbed into the driver's seat.

She opened her mouth to speak, but he grabbed the microphone off the dash and depressed a button. ''I need a tow truck on Highway 7, eighteen miles south of town. Car's in a ditch. Tell Pete he can wait till the storm passes. I've picked up the driver.''

"Ten-four," a no-nonsense female voice replied. "Need medical assistance?"

"Negative." The sheriff gave a call number, signed off and replaced the microphone on the dash.

Warmth from the heater was slowly thawing Jessica, and either the bump on her head or the welcomed heat was making her drowsy. She seemed to be floating, a state she'd experienced only once before, when she'd drunk too much champagne at Max's New Year's Eve party last January. In such a blissful state, she found maintaining a good head of steam over her situation difficult.

And ignoring the attributes of the man next to her impossible.

She'd sworn off men, she reminded herself, except as the occasional dinner date, although Max never gave up playing matchmaker, hoping she'd find the right man and settle down to raise a family. Having witnessed the chaos and heartbreak that emotional entanglements had created in her parents' lives, she wanted none of it. Her life was full enough as it was. She had her fantastic job, her South Beach condo, her friends. She didn't need love or anything slightly resembling it. She'd avoided infatuations as fiercely as she avoided accounting errors. She'd never had a broken heart, never shed a tear over a man, never sat by the phone for a call that never came....

Never intended to.

"Now—" The sheriff, who appeared even more attractive at close range than he had in the bank, turned to her. "Want me to take you back to the hotel?"

Even in its groggy state, her mind somehow continued to function. If she went back to town, she'd have to rent another car, drive the same treacherous roads and arrive hours, if not an entire day, later than she'd planned. And she had no intention of remaining in Montana a day longer than she had to. She hated the dinky little town, the monotony of the landscape, and, most of all, the intolerably frigid weather.

To plead her case, she lifted her lips in what she hoped was an alluring smile. "I don't suppose you could take me to the Shooting Star Ranch?"

He started the engine and put the car into gear. "Sure you don't want to have a doctor check you out? You must have been shaken up pretty bad."

"Nothing a few aspirin won't cure."

He gave her a quick head-to-toe glance as if to assure himself. "Then the Shooting Star Ranch it is." He pulled onto the highway and drove slowly through the swirling snow as confidently as if he knew the route blindfolded. "You're not used to driving in these conditions."

She resented his implication that the accident had been her fault, and that irritable feeling helped squelch any danger of succumbing to his aw-shucks Western charm. "I was doing fine until someone sideswiped me and knocked me off the road."

"They didn't stop?"

She could hear the anger in his voice and was glad

it wasn't directed at her. "If they did, I was unconscious. No one was around when I came to."

"Get a license-plate number?"

She shook her head and winced at the pain the movement caused. "All I saw was a dark-colored pickup with tinted windows."

He stifled another curse. "You've just described ninety percent of the vehicles in this county." Flicking her a glance that seemed to pierce straight through her, he asked, "You sure you were hit? I can't believe no one stopped to help, especially in this weather. People here are friendlier than that."

"Have the garage check the car's driver's-side panels." She didn't like his suggesting that she'd lied, and the frost in her voice matched the temperature outside. "The damage has to be there. Whoever it was, hit me hard. Twice."

This time he seemed to accept her account. "I'll ask for a paint sample from the damaged area. See if I can track the truck down."

"Isn't that a lot of trouble for a fender bender?" His thoroughness impressed her.

"Hit-and-run's bad enough." His scowl emphasized the rugged contours of his face. "If you'd frozen to death back there, it would also have been manslaughter. At least."

"At least?"

"If someone ran you off the road on purpose and you'd died from the accident or the cold, it would have been homicide."

She shook her head, unable to comprehend the notion that the wreck had been intended. The movement was not a smart reaction, with her head and body still painfully sore. ''Do all sheriffs think like you?''

''How's that?''

''Paranoid. I've only been in town a few hours. Who would want to run me off the road, much less murder me?''

''Ever heard of road rage?'' His expression was dead serious, and she couldn't decide if he was better looking when he smiled or was solemn. ''The perpetrators seldom know their victims.''

''I didn't have time to do anything to make him mad. This guy came out of nowhere.''

''Anyone else you've ticked off since you came to town?''

''Nobody but the shotgun Santa.'' Her eyes widened at a sudden thought. ''You haven't released him, have you?''

''No way.''

''Has he robbed other banks?''

The sheriff's tanned forehead wrinkled in a frown. ''The guy has no record. Holds a respectable job in Grange County north of us. He isn't on drugs. In fact, he doesn't fit the profile of a bank robber at all. And whatever his motive, he's not talking.''

''Maybe the coming holidays affected his reasoning. Not everybody's crazy about Christmas,'' Jessica said with more intensity than she'd intended.

The knock on her head had made her talkative. She rarely felt so at ease with strangers. "Maybe he was... What do the psychologists call it? Acting out?"

"We're still running a check on him. All we know for certain is that he wasn't the one who ran you off the road. Anybody else who might be out to get you?"

Jessica could think of dozens, business executives whose get-rich-quick-at-someone-else's-expense schemes she'd thwarted with her investigations. But none of them was within a thousand miles of Montana.

Unless...

"I haven't met the people at Shooting Star Ranch yet," she said. "Don't know if someone there has something to hide, something they're afraid my audit might unearth."

The sheriff coughed harshly, as if something had caught suddenly in his throat. Once he was able to speak again, he gave her a megawatt smile that warmed her more than the superefficient car heater. "Guess you won't know that until you meet them and do your homework."

He seemed remarkably unconcerned.

"Do you know them?" Jessica asked. "You don't think they're a threat to me?"

His expression sobered, but mischief twinkled in his brown eyes. "I'll give you my number, so you can call if you feel threatened."

Being around the sheriff was making her paranoid, expecting criminals around every corner, she thought, when probably she'd simply been the victim of ugly but common road rage. "Maybe the guy who hit me was drunk, and I was merely in the wrong place at the wrong time."

"Maybe." He slowed the car, turned off the highway and stopped in front of a rustic timber arch, where the words Shooting Star Ranch and the emblem of a star with lines trailing behind it like a comet's tail had been burned into the sign above the driveway. "We're here."

Jessica peered through the snow. "Where's the house?"

The sheriff started the car again. "Five miles up this road."

"Five miles! That's a heck of a driveway."

"Short by Montana standards, but don't worry. I'll deposit you safely at the front door."

They continued up the driveway with snow-covered open fields on either side. After several minutes, dark shadows loomed in front of them. As they approached, Jessica could make out tall, leafless trees in front of a huge, three-story Victorian house, complete with symmetrical Queen Anne turrets flanking spacious porches.

"This is the main house," the sheriff announced.

"It's not what I expected."

"Not every ranch looks like the Ponderosa," he said with a wry grin.

When the sheriff brought the SUV to a halt, Jessica could see the Shooting Star emblem carved into the corbels and cornices of the gingerbread trim.

"It lives up to its name." She turned to the sheriff and offered her hand. "I don't know how to thank you. You've saved my life. Twice now."

He gripped her hand firmly in the calloused warmth of his own. "All in a day's work. We serve and protect."

"And provide delivery service." She kept her voice light and retracted her hand, unwilling to admit how much she'd enjoyed the contact, how much she liked him. Her attraction to him wouldn't be a problem, however, since she'd never see him again. "I'll just hop out and get my luggage. No need to inconvenience you more than I already have."

He killed the engine and opened his door. "I'll get your bag."

Jessica climbed out quickly and met him at the back of the SUV. "It isn't heavy. I can manage. You need to get back to work."

"No problem. I'm through for the day."

She reached for the luggage, unwilling to obligate herself more to a man she found entirely too appealing. "Then you should be headed home."

He took the case from her. "I am home."

She stopped short. "What?"

He grinned and gestured toward the front door. "I'm Ross McGarrett. My family owns Shooting Star Ranch. Welcome, Ms. Landon."

ROSS COULDN'T HELP GRINNING even wider at Jessica Landon's look of surprise. He'd had a hard enough time keeping from laughing earlier when she'd suggested that someone at the ranch might be out to get her. More likely she'd want to kill *him* when she saw the state of the ranch's books. Nothing illegal or sinister. Just absolute, unfettered chaos. He hated paperwork worse than criminals.

Before he could say more, however, the front door swung open, and the light from the hall outlined a tall, regal figure peering into the darkness and swirling snow. "Ross, is that you?"

Beside him, Jessica's mouth dropped open, but she snapped it shut quickly when she caught him watching her. He didn't blame her for the reaction. His grandmother had that effect on people. Meeting her was like meeting the queen. Fiona had grown up in Manhattan, attended the best Eastern finishing schools, traveled throughout Europe and the Far East, and inherited a small fortune before she'd married his grandfather and moved to the West. After all these years in the wilds of Montana, the polished cosmopolitan aura still clung to her, from her elegant sense of style and her cultured voice and accent to her stately posture and expression, all attributes that camouflaged a heart as immense as the Big Sky State.

"It's me, Fiona," he called to his grandmother, "and I have Ms. Landon with me." Taking Jessica's elbow with one hand, her bag with the other, he helped her up the broad icy steps into the house.

"Welcome, Ms. Landon," Fiona said. "We've been expecting you. I'm glad you're both here safe and sound, Ross. There's a blizzard coming."

Jessica looked surprised and cocked her head toward the door. "What we came through wasn't a blizzard?"

Fiona shook her head. "The weather's mild now compared to a real storm."

Jessica shook off her surprise and became the professional, competent woman he'd first noticed in the bank. "Then it's good I'm here so I can begin work right away."

Ross had to give her credit. She'd been caught in the middle of a bank holdup, shot at, and run off the road, all in one day, yet none of her troubles seemed to have daunted her. The woman was either an incurable workaholic or had nerves of steel. Or both.

Jessica's small stature and fragile beauty were deceiving. When Fiona had told him she'd engaged a top financial consultant from Miami, Ross had expected an Ivy League male with a button-down collar, expensive suit, a sharp mind and an eagle eye for details. The lovely Jessica had been a pleasing surprise.

On the one hand.

On the other, bad enough having another man chastise Ross for his sloppy bookkeeping. He could only imagine the disdain the superefficient Ms. Landon would have for his records.

And on another hand—

"No need to start work tonight," Fiona was saying graciously. "Come into the living room. We'll have a glass of wine before dinner."

"Maybe Ms. Landon would like to see her room and settle in first," Ross suggested, catching sight of Jessica's ruined stockings. "She's had a rough day."

"Of course," his grandmother replied. "The guest suite's ready. Will you take her bag?"

Jessica reached for her luggage. "I can manage—"

"Nonsense," Fiona said in that tone of hers that squelched any argument. "Ross doesn't mind."

Ross hefted the suitcase, which, judging from its weight, couldn't possibly hold enough clothing for December on the Montana prairie. Then again, Jessica probably expected to spend the entire time indoors with her very pretty head buried in his accounts.

"Your room's upstairs," he said. "I'm right behind you."

Jessica started up the stairs and Ross followed, unable to keep his eyes off the sculpted curve of her calves, the slender turn of her ankles, the subtle swing of her shapely behind. For such a small package, she certainly packed a wallop. She mesmerized him more than any woman ever had. Which was unfortunate. The last thing he needed now was a distraction from his job.

"This is it." He indicated a doorway on the right, halfway down the hall, waited for her to enter, and followed inside with her bag.

Jessica gazed around the room, her eyes alight with approval. "It's beautiful."

Seeing the room through her eyes, as if for the first time, Ross agreed. A fire burned cheerfully in the fireplace with comfortable chairs grouped in front of it. Piles of pillows edged with lace were heaped at the head of the four-poster mahogany bed. "Fiona uses all her favorite antiques in here. I hope you'll be comfortable."

"Do you always call your grandmother Fiona?" Jessica asked.

Ross nodded. "She never liked to be called grandma. Said it made her feel old and dowdy."

"She's definitely neither," Jessica noted. "She's an impressive woman."

He placed Jessica's bag on an eighteenth-century blanket chest at the foot of the bed. "Bathroom's through the door on the left. Closet's on the right. Join us downstairs when you're ready."

"Thank you. I won't be long." Looking only slightly dazed, especially in light of all she'd been through, Jessica closed the door behind him when he left.

Ross hurried down the stairs and found Fiona in the living room in her favorite chair by the fire.

"Where's Courtney?" he asked.

"She's asleep," Fiona said. "I fed her early. She was completely tired out."

Ross gazed at his grandmother with concern. "I wish you'd let me hire someone to look after her. I'm afraid she's too much for you."

"The day a two-year-old is too much," Fiona said with a grimace, "you'll have to hire someone to look after *me*."

He'd had this argument and lost many times before, so he went on to the subject weighing most heavily on his mind.

"You didn't tell me Rinehart and Associates were sending a woman," he said in an accusing tone, one he'd seldom used with his grandmother.

"Jessica Landon is the best at what she does, according to Max Rinehart," Fiona replied easily, apparently unperturbed by his disapproval. She reached for the novel on the table beside her chair, her usual signal that the current discussion was closed.

"It's not her accounting skills that concern me." He paused, reluctant to report bad news. "It's happening again."

Her hand froze in midair at the grimness in his tone, and the color left her face. "You're certain?"

Ross shrugged. "Not a hundred percent, but a man would be better able to take care of himself."

Fiona closed her eyes as if gathering strength, then opened them again. "Another accident?"

"She was run off the road. Said a pickup slammed

into her car twice and kept going. Didn't sound like an accident. And she'd have frozen to death if I hadn't come along.''

"You have to tell her. Warn her.''

Ross nodded. "But not tonight. She's been through enough already today. And she's perfectly safe here.''

Fiona compressed her lips and shook her head. "When is this going to stop?''

Ross sank into the seat across from her, weariness seeping through his bones. "Not until I catch the killer.''

Chapter Three

Jessica surveyed the pleasant room with relief. She'd had visions of sleeping in the rustic equivalent of a bunkhouse, but the McGarrett guest room would rival any suite in Miami's finest luxury hotels. In addition to an arrangement of pale pink roses and stargazer lilies in a cut-crystal vase, a silver bowl filled with fruit, a box of Godiva chocolates and three books from the latest bestseller list topped the table between two inviting overstuffed chairs centered in front of the fireplace.

Judging from the expensive antique furnishings and the lavish appointments in the room, the McGarretts weren't hurting for money, Jessica thought. Then she recalled how deceiving appearances could be. Many people who'd lost every cent often continued to put up a good front. Only time and the careful scrutiny of the ranch's books would reveal the true status of the McGarrett finances.

She longed for a hot bath to soothe her bruises but was unwilling to keep her formidable hostess waiting. Wishing fleetingly for warm wool socks, Jessica changed her stockings, stripped off her sodden clothes and dressed in a navy-blue skirt, white silk blouse and a camel-colored cashmere cardigan. She slipped her feet into low-heeled shoes, which were blessedly dry.

A few minutes later, she joined Fiona and Ross in the living room downstairs. Fiona set aside the book she'd been reading and glanced up with a smile of greeting that reached to her brilliant green eyes.

The woman could have been a fashion model, even at her age, Jessica thought, with her magnificent white hair arranged in Gibson girl fashion that matched the period of her house. Fiona's fine bone structure, easy grace and sense of style, even in casual clothes, would fit perfectly on any couturier's runway in Paris or Rome.

Ross pushed to his feet from the opposite chair. The big man would have overpowered an average-size room, but not this expansive space with its ten-foot ceilings. Jessica was struck again by his attractiveness. Not the cultured beauty of his grandmother, but a raw, earthy appeal that set her senses tingling. His expression, like Fiona's, was welcoming, but with a hint of reserve. Jessica wondered how the sheriff felt about having a stranger living in his house, scrutinizing his finances and making the ultimate recommendation on whether the Shooting Star would be his.

"Bring us a glass of wine, please, Ross." Fiona gestured Jessica to sit in the chair across from hers.

Ross looked at Jessica. "What would you like?"

"Whatever Mrs. McGarrett's having will be fine."

"Call me Fiona," the older woman said. "And tell me all about Max. How is he?"

"You know Max?" Jessica didn't know why she felt surprised. Her amiable boss seemed to be acquainted with half the population of the United States.

Fiona smiled, and the expression softened the majestic planes of her face. "We grew up near each other in New York. Our families were friends."

Ross handed Jessica a glass of white wine, and his big hand brushed hers. With dismay, she realized she not only hadn't seen the last of the too-charming sheriff, but she was going to be living in the same house with him. For days on end.

Concentrate on business, she ordered herself, *and Ross McGarrett won't be a problem.*

She returned her attention to Fiona, but remained aware of Ross, pouring himself a whiskey over ice at the antique sideboard that served as a bar.

"Max is well," she told her hostess, "and looking forward to his grandchildren coming home for the holidays."

"You understand your assignment here?" Fiona asked.

"Max explained everything," Jessica said.

Ross sank onto a sofa nearby, stretched his long

legs in front of him and sipped his whiskey. Although he seemed nonchalant, Jessica could tell he was taking in every word of their conversation. She struggled to concentrate on what Fiona was saying.

"Please indulge me," Fiona said, "and let me restate what I want you to do."

"You?" Jessica asked in surprise. "I've been hired by the trustees."

"I am the trustee," Fiona said.

"There's only one?" Jessica asked.

Fiona dipped her head in her regal fashion. "Since my husband died ten years ago."

"I see," Jessica said, even though she thought the entire arrangement odd.

"I'm sure you find the circumstances of the trust…unusual," Fiona stated, as if reading her mind.

Jessica glanced at Ross, who was studying the ice in his glass, before returning her gaze to Fiona. "It's not my job to assess the legal contract, only to fulfill the financial obligations of it."

Fiona nodded in approval. "Ross's great-great-grandfather set up a trust to make certain the ranch remained intact and in the family. Every McGarrett's done the same since. When the current owner dies, the heir goes through a period of…I guess you could call it apprenticeship for ten years. After that time, if he's proved himself capable of operating the ranch to its maximum capacity, the trustees award him ownership."

"And if he hasn't?" Jessica asked.

"The ranch is owned and operated by the trust," Ross said, "until the next generation of McGarretts has a chance to prove themselves."

The next generation, Jessica thought with a start. She hadn't considered that the handsome sheriff was probably married. With children. Relief surged through her. She was uninterested in men, and she was even less interested in *married* men. If a wife and kiddies were present, Jessica wouldn't have to worry about Ross's charm and could concentrate on her work without distraction.

"The trust is a formality," Ross continued. "There's never been a McGarrett who didn't inherit."

A worried frown scudded across Fiona's strong features, but she quickly regained her composure. His grandmother's fleeting expression made Jessica wonder if Ross was in danger of breaking that record. Jessica would be the one who determined if he was operating the ranch to its maximum efficiency and whether he should assume ownership.

She took a deep breath and forced her aching muscles to relax. If Ross's management of the Shooting Star didn't meet standards, she'd be the bearer of the bad news. The prospect wasn't pleasant, even though she'd handled such situations before, but disappointing the appealing man who'd twice saved her life wasn't something she liked to contemplate.

Fiona gazed at Ross with concern clouding her green eyes. He didn't meet his grandmother's gaze, and the knuckles of his hand were white where he gripped his glass.

In spite of the McGarretts' hospitality and obvious efforts to put Jessica at ease, she could sense a tension in the room, an underlying current of things unsaid, fears unstated, and she wondered at their source.

"Will the storm be a problem?" Jessica thought the vicious weather might be the cause of her hosts' unspoken anxiety.

"The cattle have weathered bigger storms than what's forecast," Ross said, apparently unconcerned over his herd. "The worst should blow over during the night."

The blast of wind against the side of the house rattled the windows, making Jessica believe the worst had already arrived. Not that the wind frightened her. She'd ridden out hurricanes in Miami. What concerned her was being stranded with strangers, no matter how hospitable they appeared.

"And we have a generator if we lose power," Fiona assured her. "You mustn't be alarmed."

Jessica drank her wine. If the weather didn't have them on edge, what did? Her instincts were flashing on yellow alert, cues that in the past had cautioned her to look beyond the financial statistics when evaluating a situation. Something was troubling the McGarretts. Only time would tell whether their anxiety was related to Jessica's assignment or something altogether different.

"Have you worked for Max long?" Fiona asked.

"Since I finished graduate school," Jessica said, "eight years ago."

"Then you must be only a few years younger than Ross," the older woman observed.

"Now, Fiona," Ross cautioned gently, his deep voice seductively edged with a cowboy twang. "You know better than to mention a woman's age."

"Nonsense," Fiona said. "I'll be seventy-nine in March and proud of it. Why should anyone be ashamed of living long and well?"

Jessica hastened to change the subject. "I'd like to begin work as soon as possible."

"Of course," Fiona answered. "But not until after dinner. No one can work on an empty stomach."

"I can work while I eat," Jessica suggested. "Just a sandwich and some coffee on a tray—"

"Nonsense," Fiona repeated with an indignant frown. "You're our guest. Dinner will be ready in a few minutes. You can begin when we've finished."

Ross glanced at Jessica over the rim of his glass with a sympathetic smile and an it-won't-help-to-argue look.

At the same time, an elderly man with Far Eastern features and wearing a white chef's jacket appeared in the doorway.

"Dinner is served, Mrs. McGarrett," he announced in a heavily accented voice, then disappeared down the hallway toward what Jessica assumed was the kitchen.

Jessica set her wineglass aside and stood when

Fiona did. If the woman insisted on treating her like a guest rather than an employee, Jessica didn't know how she would get any work done. She wanted to finish her assignment and go home. Back to the warmth and familiarity of Miami.

And away from the alluring charm of Sheriff Ross McGarrett before she broke her own rules about emotional involvement.

FROM HIS PLACE at the foot of the mahogany dining table, Ross studied his grandmother, seated at the head of the table, and tried to assess her motives. Fiona's gracious hospitality was usually tinged with a subtle aloofness, but she'd dropped her customary reserve around Jessica. Maybe her warmth toward their guest was the result of sympathy for Jessica's harrowing experiences. Or simply an extension of her friendship with Max Rinehart, her childhood friend. Whatever the reason, his grandmother was treating Jessica as if she were practically a member of the family.

Ross hadn't become successful as a sheriff without learning to read people well, however, and he couldn't help feeling something else besides sympathy or old friendship was going on behind his grandmother's bright green eyes. Fiona was up to something, and not knowing what she was scheming made him uneasy. When Fiona set her mind to something, the rest of the world—and Ross in particular—had better watch out.

''My compliments to your chef. The sirloin tips are extraordinary.'' Jessica, seated between Ross and Fiona, was the epitome of politeness, but Ross could sense undercurrents in her, too. Remarkably self-possessed, even after a day that would have driven a strong man to some serious drinking, she couldn't quite hide her impatience to be about her work.

Maybe she had a family at home in Miami and she was anxious to return to them for the holidays. She wasn't wearing an engagement or wedding ring, but that fact meant nothing in today's business world. It seemed improbable such a gorgeous creature didn't have a husband or a lover eager for her return.

Jessica Landon was definitely a contradiction in terms. A strong personality resided in that tiny, fragile form. She'd handled being shot at, then sideswiped and stranded in near-zero temperatures without hysterics. With her sun-streaked auburn hair, startling blue eyes and honey-golden tan, she was a living work of art. With a mind, evidently, judging from her competency in her profession, as efficient and analytical as any computer. Her strictly business manner was certainly at odds with the emotions she generated in Ross. With a blink of surprise, he found himself remembering how she'd felt in his arms and wondering whether he'd enjoy kissing her.

He squelched that thought instantly. Just being in the McGarrett employ was dangerous enough for Jessica. Ross didn't want to endanger her further by having anyone believe he had feelings for her. Which he didn't, he assured himself. He hardly knew the woman.

But he'd sure like to know her better.

"The storm should pass by morning," Fiona was saying, "and crews will have the roads cleared by the next day. Saturday's Ross's day off, so he can show you the ranch."

Alarm flashed across Jessica's heart-shaped face, and Ross took pity on her. "Not on horseback," he assured her. "We'll take the SUV. It has four-wheel drive."

"I can ride if you'd rather," she said.

"Didn't know folks went in for horses in Miami," Ross commented, unable to hide his surprise.

"I learned at boarding school," Jessica said. "If I seemed reluctant, it isn't about riding. It's about taking time away from my work."

"Nonsense," Fiona insisted. "Seeing the ranch and how it operates is part of your job. And Ross will be happy to show off the Shooting Star."

"You must be anxious to get home for the holidays," Ross said.

Jessica patted her mouth delicately with the fine linen napkin. "Not really."

His statement hadn't prompted any revelations so he tried again, this time taking a more blunt approach. "Is your family in Miami?"

"My mother and father both live in Europe," Jessica said, adding with a small grimace, "although, not together."

''I think,'' Fiona commented with a wicked gleam in her eyes, ''what my grandson wants to know is if you're married.''

Ross choked on a bite of sirloin and coughed to clear his throat.

Jessica, cool as a mountain spring, turned her blue-eyed gaze on him and waited for his spasm to pass.

''Is my marital status relevant to my assignment?'' she asked with seeming innocence.

''It's the law officer in me.'' Ross hoped his excuse would cover his grandmother's bluntness. ''Makes me curious about people.''

Jessica's eyes twinkled and a smile tugged at the corner of her mouth, resurrecting Ross's thoughts of kissing her. ''I don't have a rap sheet, if that's what you're worried about.''

''I should say not,'' Fiona said heatedly. ''Max Rinehart wouldn't stand for it.''

Turning from Ross to Fiona, Jessica launched into an anecdote about Max teaching his oldest grandson to windsurf. Ross was so entranced by the lilting cadence of her voice, he didn't realize until long after she'd concluded her story that she'd effectively side-stepped both his and his grandmother's inquiries.

Jessica was a paradox. And a puzzle. He'd never met a woman who so willingly passed up an opportunity to talk about herself. He considered her reticence a challenge, one he was ready to meet.

''We'll need the name and number of your next

of kin," Ross told her. "Just in case of an emergency while you're staying with us."

"An emergency?" She smiled so sweetly, he knew without a doubt she was toying with him. "You mean like being shot at by bank robbers or run off the road and left to freeze to death? How many more emergencies can I expect?"

"We really live a very quiet life here," Fiona said quickly. "The emergency number is just routine."

"You can always contact Max." Jessica had smoothly avoided once again revealing any personal information.

Just as Ross was beginning to wonder if she had something to hide, she spoke again. "Forgive me. I don't mean to appear rude, but I always make a point of separating my professional and personal life. Your hospitality is gracious and appreciated, but I have to remain impersonal and objective to do my job appropriately."

Ross bristled at her words. "You think I'm trying to influence your report?"

"I didn't mean to offend you." Her face flushed. "I should have stressed that I have to make certain my own feelings don't color my conclusions."

"That's an exemplary attitude," Fiona said soothingly, "but it shouldn't preclude your enjoying yourself as our guest."

Jessica looked as if she wanted to say more, but didn't.

Chang Soo removed the dinner plates and brought

in dessert. Ross finished off his crème brûlée in three bites and wished for something more substantial, like a hunk of warm huckleberry pie topped with ice cream. His grandmother, however, had always insisted on ''civilized'' dining, especially when guests were present. Ross caught the old cook's eye as he refilled Fiona's coffee cup, and Chang Soo winked, his customary signal that he'd set aside something extra for Ross in the kitchen.

Fiona drank her coffee and laid her napkin beside her plate. ''I know Jessica is anxious to begin, Ross. Why don't you show her your office?''

Jessica pushed hastily to her feet. ''Thank you for a wonderful dinner, Mrs. McGarrett.''

Ross left the dining room with Jessica on his heels and motioned her to precede him down the hall toward the rear of the house. At the last door on his left, he reached around her, catching the tantalizing exotic fragrance of her shampoo once again, and opened the door to his office with a flourish.

He stepped back for her to enter first and stopped short at her gasp of surprise.

''Your office!'' Her low, sultry voice had risen an octave in alarm. ''Someone's vandalized it!''

Chapter Four

Jessica stared at Ross's home office in dazed disbelief. Max had always insisted bad luck came in threes. Today she'd experienced a bank robbery and a car accident. The total disarray of the records she was supposed to examine was a third tragedy, a bitterly disappointing ending to a perfectly awful day.

Piles of papers littered the antique rolltop desk and floor, and ledgers were scattered haphazardly across the room. Desk and file drawers stood open, their contents spilling in chaos onto the Navajo rug.

"Who would have done this?" Jessica felt a whopper of a tension headache coming on, adding to the pounding her head had already suffered from the accident. She hoped she'd remembered to pack her Extra Strength Tylenol.

She jumped, startled when Ross took her elbow, steered her around file folders stacked in leaning piles on the floor to a deep leather chair and motioned her to sit. He seemed unbelievably calm for a man whose office had just been trashed. Dealing on a daily basis with lawbreakers and the devastating results of their crimes must have given him nerves of steel.

"Who would have done this?" He repeated her query in a reasonable tone, folded his long legs and sank into the matching chair across from hers. "I did."

She shook her head to clear the fog, thinking she hadn't heard him correctly. "You vandalized your own office?"

His slow grin, a mixture of sheepishness and amusement, and the effect it had on her pulse only added to her confusion. Had he purposely intended to sabotage her work? And if so, why?

"I had planned to clean things up before you arrived," he explained. "In fact, I was headed home for that very reason when the bank was held up today."

She cocked her head and regarded him with suspicion. "You mean this disaster wasn't deliberate?"

"Let's just say my filing system leaves something to be desired."

Jessica surveyed the room with dismay. Her job would be hard enough with everything neat and in order. She'd hoped to return to Miami before Christmas. Now, as she surveyed the chaos that surrounded her, Easter seemed a more likely target date.

Her expression must have given away her distress, because Ross leaned forward in his chair, big hands clasped between his knees, his brown eyes alight with apology. "I'm not good at clerical work under the best of circumstances, but this past year has been worse than usual. I'm sorry for the mess I've left you to deal with."

Worry creased the handsome plane of his forehead, and for the first time, she noted the hint of exhaustion in the slight slump of his broad shoulders. She struggled to keep her focus on business. "The ranch has had a rough year?"

She hoped the financial toll on the ranch hadn't been too high. In spite of her best intentions to remain objective, she couldn't help liking Ross McGarrett. She wanted to be able to recommend the transfer of the Shooting Star into his name.

He shook his head, and a lock of thick brown hair fell over his forehead, giving him a boyish look that made him even more appealing. "The ranch is fine. You'll figure that out for yourself—" he tossed her a twisted smile of apology "—if you're able to plow through the mess I've made here."

Curiosity momentarily thrust aside her concerns over the paperwork pandemonium that surrounded her, but she stopped herself from asking prying questions. To obtain unbiased results, she had to keep her distance from the client. She couldn't allow herself to become entangled in his personal problems.

"You wouldn't think Swenson County would be a hotbed of crime," Ross said with a shake of his head, as if he couldn't believe it himself. "But ever since SCOFF raised its ugly head, we've had more problems than this part of the country's seen since Prohibition.''

Crime had an effect on the economic climate of a region and would be relevant to her report, so Jessica allowed herself to ask questions. ''What's 'scoff'?''

Ross grimaced, as if he'd tasted something rotten. ''An acronym for Swenson County Freedom Fighters.''

''Freedom fighters? What freedom are they fighting for?''

''Freedom from government interference in their lives—or so they claim. What they're really after is freedom to do as they damn well please. They're anarchists, plain and simple.''

''And they've broken the laws?''

Ross leaned back in his chair with a sigh of frustration. ''I wish I knew.''

''You're the sheriff. If you don't know, who does?''

''Ever since this group distributed their manifesto on leaflets dropped around town, there's been an increase in crimes—breaking and entering, assaults on government officials from judges to councilmen—''

''But not on law enforcement?''

His eyes darkened until they were almost black. ''Not directly.''

She waited, hoping he would explain, but he merely continued his previous track. ''We've had a string of bank robberies—''

''You think Santa's a member of SCOFF?''

He shrugged, his face grim. "So far, we have no way to tie him to the group. There's also been at least one murder I'm pretty sure can be laid at SCOFF's doorstep."

Ross's eyes blazed with indignation and resolve, and Jessica was glad she'd done nothing to set the determined man in front of her on *her* trail.

"So you've arrested them?" she asked.

He snorted in disgust. "Might as well try to arrest smoke. It's an ultrasecret group. We haven't been able to identify a single member so far, much less pin anything on them. And they're clever. More clever than the average criminal. When they commit a crime, they leave few, if any, clues behind."

"Can't the people they've assaulted identify them?" In such a small community, Jessica couldn't understand how any group could remain anonymous.

"They wear disguises. Plus they attack their victims in deserted areas where no one else is around, so there's never an eyewitness. By the time help arrives, the perpetrators are long gone." He appeared to grow wearier as he spoke. "The psychological effect of their crimes is wearing my department down. People are asking why these criminals aren't being caught. Wondering if we're competent to do the job."

"Are you?" The question popped out before she could stop it, but Ross seemed undisturbed by her bluntness.

"I have the best team of deputies in the state.

What we're up against is domestic terrorism. Because these SCOFFers are local, they know how to hit and run, where to flee and hide. And they blend into the landscape and the community because they've always lived here.''

''You're sure of that?''

Ross pushed his fingers through his hair. ''As sure as I can be of anything about their craziness. Somebody's mad as hell at the local authorities. Swenson County's not the center of the universe, so it makes sense the lawbreakers are local.''

''As small as the population is, wouldn't the process of elimination help?'' Jessica suggested.

''You'd think so,'' Ross said with a sigh, ''but so far, we don't have one good suspect. We have so many characters here, people who go their own way and make their own rules—that's why they like living here in the middle of nowhere—that if eccentricity pointed the finger, two-thirds of the county would be suspect.''

''So what do you do?''

''We wait. Sooner or later, whoever's behind these crimes will grow overconfident. He or she—or they—will slip up and make a mistake. It won't have to be a big one. Just enough to put us on the right trail. Then we'll have them.''

Jessica could sense how his responsibility toward the citizens of Swenson County weighed on him. She also wondered how he found time to run the Shooting Star, a question she would have to raise in her report.

Ross straightened in his chair and squared his shoulders. ''Our local crime spree, however, isn't your problem.'' He waved his hand, encompassing the room with his gesture. ''But this mess is. I'll get started on it now.''

''Tell me how I can help.'' Jessica assured herself it wasn't concern for the clearly bone-tired sheriff but her eagerness to complete her assignment that motivated her.

He scratched his head and surveyed the room as if contemplating a puzzle. ''If you have a suggestion, I'm open to it.''

Jessica rose and picked up the nearest loose paper, a receipt for cattle feed bought the previous year. ''First, we group everything by year—''

The door of the office banged open, and a blur of golden curls and pink flannel nightgown streaked inside and scrambled onto Ross's lap. ''Daddy, Daddy!''

Ross cuddled the toddler, and the little girl wrapped her arms around his neck and planted a sloppy kiss on his lips. Jessica felt a strange twinge in her heart at the picture they made, a tiny tot and a gentle giant of a man, obviously devoted to each other.

Ross kissed the child back, then settled her on his lap and gazed at her as if he couldn't get enough of her. ''Granny said you were asleep.''

"I waked up." The toddler's eyes, the same soft gray as pussy willows, caught sight of Jessica, and the girl turned suddenly shy, hiding her face against Ross's shirt.

"This is Miss Landon," Ross said. "She'll be staying with us for a while."

The toddler, obviously uncomfortable around strangers, peeked at Jessica with one eye.

"This is Courtney," Ross explained. "She's usually in bed by now."

"Hi, Courtney." Jessica felt a sinking feeling in her stomach and hoped her work would keep her out of the little girl's way. Jessica knew nothing about children and found Courtney even more intimidating than the incredible mess in Ross's office.

"Wanna make a snowman," Courtney said, momentarily ignoring Jessica to plead her case with Ross. "A big one."

"We'll have to wait until tomorrow," Ross said easily. "It's dark outside now. Maybe tomorrow Miss Landon will help you."

Jessica felt the color leave her face. She'd traveled to exotic foreign countries, tackled strange languages and customs, but she'd never had to navigate through the unknown territory of dealing with children. Not even with Max's grandchildren, who'd been well into adolescence when she entered his firm.

And as for playing in the snow, she'd sooner have a root canal. Only now were her feet thawing from her previous exposure to the cold. She couldn't be happier if she didn't have to leave the house until it was time to drive to the airport for her flight home to warm, sunny Florida.

Courtney's puckered face expressed the doubts Jessica felt. Her little-girl radar must have picked up on her guest's misgivings. "Want you, Daddy."

"I'll help," Ross promised. "Right after I show Miss Landon the ranch."

"Can I come?" Courtney batted her eyelashes at her father, a maneuver that had apparently worked well for her in the past.

"Not tomorrow, Cupcake," Ross said.

"I not Cupcake," the girl insisted. "I Cour'ney."

"You're my Courtney Cupcake," Ross said, "and it's too cold for you to be outside for as long as it'll take to show Ms. Landon the ranch."

Good thinking, Jessica thought. *Too cold for me to be outside that long, too.* But her job included an assessment of the property, and Max wouldn't accept anything but a thorough report. She wondered if the general store she'd seen in town carried thermal underwear.

"Besides," Ross was saying to the girl, "if you go with us, who would stay with Granny?"

Courtney thought for a moment. "Okay."

As if summoned by the mention of her name, Fiona appeared at the doorway. "I thought I heard that little scamp. What are you doing out of bed?"

Courtney climbed onto her knees and hugged Ross again. "Kissing Daddy good night."

The scene touched Jessica. The child plainly adored her father, and Ross was smitten with his young daughter. Their affection made Jessica painfully aware of the lack of love she'd had in her own life. Even as a small child, she'd received scant attention from her parents. Their indifference had created a hole in her heart she'd never been able to fill. She had to admit that Courtney was a lucky little girl, so readily loved by her father and Fiona. Jessica wondered where the girl's mother was. She hadn't been at dinner, and no mention had been made of her absence.

"Be quick," Fiona said to her great-granddaughter, but not unkindly, "so I can tuck you in again."

She cast a glance around the messy room and gave a discreet shudder at the shambles. "Now, Jessica, you know Ross's dirty little secret. He has the organizational skills of a gnat—when it comes to paperwork, that is. But he's really very good with people."

"Fiona," Ross said with an exaggerated sigh, "I wish you wouldn't talk about me as if I weren't here."

His grandmother smiled, her affection for her grandson as clear as his love for his daughter. "I haven't said anything I haven't told you a hundred times. Come along, Courtney. Good night, Ross, Jessica. I'm turning in early tonight. I'll see you in the morning."

With Courtney's hand tucked in hers, Fiona disappeared down the hall.

"Now—" Ross raked his fingers through his hair and looked around the room in confusion. "Where were we?"

"Do you have any boxes?" Jessica asked. "We'll need them to begin sorting."

"I think Chang Soo has some in the pantry," Ross said. "I'll get them."

THREE HOURS LATER, with the majority of the paperwork filed into boxes dated by year, Jessica was beginning to see what the room looked like under its avalanche of clutter. It was a handsome room, a man's room with walls paneled in honey-hued knotty pine, a butter-soft leather sofa and chairs, shelves filled not only with books, but with treasures and memorabilia—a Sioux dream catcher, several moss agates, a few rodeo trophies and a bird's nest.

A striking Ansel Adams print of rugged mountains reflected in a peaceful lake hung above the fireplace, where Ross had built a cheerful fire after clearing away the paper hazards. Jessica reached for a picture frame, facedown on the mantel, and set it upright. Ross McGarrett's handsome face stared back at her. His arm was around a young woman, barely out of her teens, who held a newborn infant in her arms.

"Your wife?" Jessica asked.

Ross glanced at the photo, and his expression was unreadable. He nodded. "That's Kathy."

"Will I meet her?"

He slumped into a chair and fought visibly against a consuming weariness. He lifted his head and met Jessica's eyes, his face etched with sadness. "Kathy died over a year ago."

Nothing like putting my foot in my mouth, Jessica thought. The man's private life was none of her business. And his dead wife was without doubt a painful subject. His loss was written all over his attractive face.

"I'm sorry," Jessica said.

He appeared to shake off his sorrow. "You've had a terrible day, and it's late. I'll finish up here. You go to bed."

Jessica almost started to argue, but her fatigue had caught up with her. She wondered how she'd find the energy to climb the stairs to the guest room. And Ross looked as tired as she felt.

"Why don't we finish this together in the morning?" she suggested, surprising herself. If she encouraged Ross to work into the night, she'd be that much further ahead tomorrow, that much closer to completing her report and returning home. But she didn't have the heart to push him. Maybe her fatigue was affecting her brain, she rationalized, and hoped a good night's sleep would make her more objective.

Any attempt at objectivity flew out the window with Ross's response. His broad smile dazzled her.

"You're sure you don't mind?" he said. "I could use some shut-eye."

"Good night." Jessica turned to leave.

Ross caught her by the hand. "You got off to a rocky start, but I hope you'll be comfortable here."

The strength of his grip and the warmth of his skin against hers sent a tingle up her arm. It had to be her tiredness making her loopy, she told herself. He was only a man after all, just Max's client, a widower she'd never see again after her work here was complete.

Then why did she have the illogical urge to feel his arms around her?

"Thanks," she said. "I'm sure everything will be fine."

Before she could entertain any more bizarre thoughts, she pulled her hand from his and hurried away.

Once in her room, she found the Tylenol, took two capsules and went to bed. When her head hit the pillow, she fell instantly asleep, but a homicidal Santa in a black pickup pursued her through her dreams.

ROSS ALWAYS ENJOYED weekend mornings. Ever since he could remember, Fiona had made them special by having Chang Soo serve spectacular breakfasts in the solarium. The two-story-high glass-enclosed addition on the southeast side of the house had been built especially for her by his grandfather. Over the years, Fiona had filled it with plants, including palms and Australian tree ferns that now towered overhead, filtering the bright early-morning light.

Fiona and Courtney were still asleep, as was their custom. Neither of the women in his life was an early riser, so Ross could enjoy the solitude of the winter morning. With a mug of strong coffee on the table in front of him, he ignored Fiona's daily copy of the *New York Times* to concentrate on the problems at hand.

Despite the fact that his department had caught yesterday's bank robber almost instantly, Ross felt little satisfaction from the arrest. His gut told him the man was somehow connected with SCOFF, but he needed hard evidence to tie him to the covert militant militia group hiding in their midst and wreaking havoc on the county. The voters had expressed no reservations about his competence as sheriff, but he was beginning to wonder about himself. Had he missed some vital clue? Had he done everything he could?

"Wow!"

Jessica's exclamation of surprise pulled him from his self-doubts. He looked up to find her standing in the entrance to the solarium, her astonishment at Fiona's favorite retreat clearly visible. Dressed in forest-green slacks with a matching jacket and a cream-colored turtleneck sweater that set off her stunning auburn hair, she could have been dining at Tavern on the Green in Central Park instead of a Montana ranch. He cast a dubious glance at her matching leather high-heeled pumps and wondered whether she had packed boots fit for riding.

"Good morning," he said.

She crossed the room toward the table tucked against the glass and craned her neck to take in the greenery that surrounded them. "This is unbelievable."

He couldn't help noticing her slight limp and a small bruise, barely concealed by makeup, on her cheekbone. He wondered what other aftereffects she had suffered from her accident. He decided that touring the ranch on horseback today was a bad idea in her present condition, especially if she hadn't been riding in a while. She probably had more than enough sore muscles already.

"Fiona's the one with the green thumb." Ross stood and pulled out a chair next to him. "She's worked miracles in here. Coffee?"

"Thanks." Jessica sat and gazed past him through the glass to the south lawn, where snowdrifts, sparkling in the sun, obscured the remnants of Fiona's summer garden.

He filled Jessica a mug from the carafe at the sideboard, topped off his own and took his seat. "You're up early."

"Habit," she confessed. Violet smudges were barely visible beneath her eyes, suggesting she hadn't slept well. Ross wasn't surprised. After the day she'd had yesterday, he doubted she'd slept at all.

"We don't have to work on my office this morning, if you'd rather rest—"

"I'd rather work." Her tension was evident, from the set of her jaw, to the tight muscles of her neck where a tiny vein pulsed, momentarily distracting him.

"Don't you ever relax?" He forced his attention away from the blood pounding beneath the smoothness of her skin.

She sipped her coffee and nodded in approval of Chang Soo's special blend. "I'll spend three weeks in St. Thomas when I'm through here."

"Another assignment?" Jessica was a workaholic if he'd ever seen one.

She surprised him by shaking her head. "Vacation."

"When was your last one?" Maybe it was the lawman in him, but he couldn't help asking questions. He wanted to find out all he could about the woman who'd be spending the next month in his house.

Her face puckered in a frown. "I can't remember."

"Then you're working too hard."

She threw him a challenging stare. "When was *your* last vacation?"

"Over a year ago, right before my wife died."

She glanced away, a pink flush staining her cheeks. "I'm sorry."

"It's a good memory," Ross said, trying to ease

her discomfort. "Fiona took Kathy, Courtney and me to New York City to show us where she grew up. Courtney was too young to appreciate it, but Kathy had a great time. I was always glad her last days were so happy."

"You must miss her a great deal."

Ross felt a twinge of guilt. Kathy hadn't been in his life long enough for him to feel the loss as deeply as he might have otherwise. "She was barely twenty, in perfect health, with a baby she adored. Her death was a tragedy."

Jessica nodded and drank her coffee.

Ross took a deep breath. He might as well tell her. She'd find out soon enough from someone. "Kathy was murdered."

Jessica's complexion paled. A thousand questions flashed in the blue of her eyes, but she gave voice to none of them.

"You're wondering who would want to kill a beautiful young wife and mother," he said.

She glanced away, her face now flushed as if embarrassed he'd read her mind. "It's none of my business."

"You'll hear all kinds of rumors," Ross said. "Since you'll be living here, you'll be more comfortable if you know the truth."

"If you'd rather not talk about it—"

"The case is an open investigation, so it's on my mind constantly."

Her eyes widened in surprise. "You haven't caught the killer?"

Ross tightened his grip around his coffee mug, an outward sign of his inner frustration. "We'd just returned from New York. I went back to work, and Kathy planned to drive into town later in the morning to buy groceries. I was at my desk when I got the call. A fatal accident on Highway 7."

Jessica frowned. "But you said she was murdered."

Ross nodded grimly. "She was. Her car left the road at Sutton's Curve. When the vehicle was inspected later, the mechanic discovered someone had tampered with the brakes."

He leaned back in his chair and momentarily closed his eyes, trying to erase the memory of the crushed car, the blond head slumped against the steering wheel, a crying Courtney safely cradled in the infant carrier in the back seat. When he opened his eyes again, Jessica was staring at him with a mixture of sympathy and disbelief.

"Her car was kept here at the ranch?" she asked.

"You're thinking someone would have noticed a stranger around the garage," Ross said.

Jessica set her mug down with a thud. "I'm not implying anyone here tampered—"

"The house was closed while we were away. Chang Soo went home to San Francisco to visit relatives. The foreman's residence and bunkhouse don't have a clear view of the garage. Anyone could have come and gone without being seen.''

"Were there no clues?'' Jessica asked. "From what I know of crime-solving—all from reading mysteries, granted—I thought a criminal always left something behind.''

He looked at her with respect. "Locard's theory. Anytime someone enters and leaves an area, he either brings something with him or takes something away.'' He frowned. The murderer was either the craftiest of villains or had remarkable luck. "We had several heavy rains during the time we were gone. Any clues were washed away. And the car was clean. Not a fingerprint anywhere. Not even a smudge.''

"Do you have a suspect?'' Jessica held up her hands quickly. "I'm sorry. I don't mean to pry.''

"It helps to talk about it,'' Ross said. "Most people, even my own homicide detectives, avoid the subject with me. Like you, they're afraid of stirring up pain. The best thing to end my pain will be to catch the killer.''

Jessica nodded. "If it helps to talk, I'm a good listener.''

"Kathy didn't have any enemies,'' Ross said, then quickly backtracked. "Except her stiff-necked, holier-than-thou family. But even her self-righteous parents would never stoop to murder.''

"You said she was driving her car,'' Jessica said. "Was she the only one who drove it?''

"If you're implying someone meant to kill me instead," Ross said, "you're on the wrong track. I never drove her car. No, Kathy was the intended victim."

"If the killer knew whose car it was."

Ross nodded. "I'm sure whoever went to that much trouble had checked things out thoroughly. But I haven't ruled out the theory that someone was trying to get at me by killing my wife."

Jessica looked thoughtful. "Those Swenson County Freedom Fighters you mentioned last night?"

"They're at the top of my list of suspects."

Chang Soo appeared in the doorway. "You ready for me to serve breakfast now?"

Ross opened his mouth to speak at the same instant the glass wall of the solarium shattered by his head.

Chapter Five

Jessica flinched as the glass exploded around her. Before she had time to register what was happening, Ross had lunged for her. He pulled her off her chair onto the floor, knocking the breath from her lungs and covering her body with his.

"Chang Soo," he yelled. "The shutters!"

Immediately, a rumble vibrated through the room, and the morning sunlight dimmed as the electronically operated storm panels lowered across what was left of the solarium glass. When the noise ceased, Ross jumped to his feet, grabbed Jessica beneath the elbows and lifted her beside him.

In the gloom created by the closed shutters, his gaze swept her from head to foot. "You okay?"

She was grateful for the support of his strong hands, the reassuring warmth of his closeness. She was shaking, as much from her unexpected close contact with Ross as from the shattering glass. She struggled for air, still breathless from surprise and the jolt of hitting the floor. "I...think so. What happened?"

Overhead lights suddenly flooded the room, and Ross pointed grimly to the glass beside the table where they'd been sitting. "Someone shot at you."

Jessica couldn't deny the entry hole was closer to where she'd been sitting than to Ross. An attack on her, however, didn't make sense. "Why me?"

Ross's expression was fierce. "Same reason someone tried to run you off the road, maybe?"

"And that is?" Today was starting out too much like yesterday, and Jessica didn't think she could survive another twenty-four hours like the previous ones.

But Ross ignored her question. He was already striding across the room, calling to Chang Soo. "Tell Fiona to take Courtney to her room, keep the draperies closed, and stay away from the windows."

The chef hurried away to fulfill his instructions.

Ross reached the phone on the far side of the solarium, picked up the receiver and punched in a number. "I want a dragnet around Shooting Star Ranch. Stop all vehicles and confiscate any rifle that's been fired recently. And send me a Crime Scene Unit on the double."

Jessica slid into the nearest chair. When Ross McGarrett took charge, he was like a force of nature. Awesome and unstoppable. She observed with admiration his quick and forceful handling of the situation. He was apparently unrattled, unlike her, who couldn't stop her hands from trembling.

After he replaced the phone in its cradle, he strode back across the room, eyed the entry hole in the glass and followed its trajectory. He pointed to a neat circle, small and precise, in the trunk of a royal palm opposite the breakfast table. "That's where we'll find the slug. If our dragnet comes up with a recently fired weapon, we'll try for a ballistics match."

He headed for the door.

"Where are you going?" Jessica found her voice wavering. She didn't want to be left alone, especially without a clue as to what had happened and who was shooting at them.

Correction.

At her, according to Ross.

"To look for tracks," Ross said. "Someone had to leave traces in all that snow."

"But he could still be out there." She felt a sudden panic at the thought of harm coming to the man she'd tried to view only as her host. "You'll be a clear target."

Ross's face was grim. "I have a job to do."

Before Jessica could protest again, he was gone. She gazed around the room in disbelief. Except for the shattered pane of glass and the claustrophobia caused by the metal storm shutters, the room was the same peaceful oasis it had been minutes earlier.

As if to emphasize that little had changed, Chang

Soo approached her. "Your breakfast will be served in the dining room, missy."

"Thank you, but never mind," Jessica said. "I'm really not hungry."

"Miss Fiona will join you there," Chang Soo said, clearly refusing to take no for an answer. "You wait there for Mr. Ross to return."

His tone was adamant, but his smile was sympathetic. Deciding that waiting with Fiona would be better than pacing her room alone, Jessica rose and followed Chang Soo to the dining room.

The heavy velvet draperies had been drawn over the bay window at one end, but the massive chandelier, cut-crystal lamps on the buffet and a cheery blaze in the fireplace chased away the gloom.

Jessica took the seat she'd occupied the previous night at dinner. Chang Soo disappeared into the kitchen, but returned a minute later with a crystal goblet.

"Mimosa," he said with a grin. "Made with more champagne than orange juice. Make you feel better right away."

Jessica took the glass from the dignified little chef and lifted it in a toast. "Here's to Ross finding the shooter."

Chang Soo nodded solemnly and returned to the kitchen.

Jessica sipped her mimosa and hoped the champagne would calm her frazzled nerves. The West was turning out to be wilder than her wildest dreams, and she intended to do something she'd never done in her career. Abandon her assignment and head straight for home.

"Good morning, Jessica." Fiona swept into the dining room like a monarch toward a throne. "Courtney's having her breakfast with Chang Soo. He'll keep a good eye on her. Are you all right?"

Jessica suppressed the urge to giggle hysterically. All right? Amazingly yes, in spite of the fact that she'd been shot at twice, wrecked her rental car and discovered her assignment the clerical equivalent of climbing Mount Everest. And she'd be even better once she saw the last of Montana.

But her misfortunes weren't Fiona McGarrett's fault, and Jessica wouldn't be rude to Max's friend and client. "I'm fine. Luckily, whoever fired wasn't a very good shot."

"Or an excellent one," Fiona said cryptically.

"What do you mean?"

"Maybe he had no intention of hitting anyone."

Jessica felt her blood pressure rising. "Why would anyone shoot into an occupied house if not to hurt someone?"

"To generate fear." Fiona accepted the mimosa Chang Soo handed her and took a drink.

"Terrorism?" Jessica asked.

Her hostess nodded. "We've seen too much of it the past year in Swenson County."

"Maybe it was an accident." Jessica could feel denial rising within her. She didn't want to acknowledge that such cruel people existed. It made the world too scary a place. "A hunter who missed his mark."

"Possibly," Fiona admitted with a smile that was obviously forced. "We'll know more when Ross returns."

Jessica wanted to ask more about the other acts of terror that had occurred in Swenson County, but at that moment, Chang Soo entered with their breakfast, golden-brown slabs of French toast surrounded by fresh fruit. The plates could have graced the cover of *Gourmet*, but Jessica's appetite was gone, killed by a single shot through the solarium window.

ROSS STOMPED THE SNOW from his boots on the front porch, then stood aside while the Crime Scene Unit exited, their hands full of equipment and evidence bags.

Don Parker, the head technician, stopped and handed Ross a small plastic bag containing a lead slug.

"Looks like a .223 caliber," Don said. "We'll run a ballistics check. See if it matches anything already in the system."

Ross nodded and gave him back the bag. "If not, it could be from any of a hundred hunting rifles used in this area."

"Maybe we'll get lucky and come up with a hit." The technician moved on toward his van.

"Yeah," Ross said with irony, "and maybe we're in for a heat wave."

He entered the house and shucked his jacket in the front hall. Following the sound of voices, he found Jessica and Fiona in the dining room. Both looked up as he entered, their expressions questioning.

For a woman who'd been targeted two days in a row, Jessica appeared amazingly composed. Only the tiny hint of white around her lips revealed her tension. Ross felt his heart warm at the sight of her. Something about the woman, whether her courage and feistiness or just the strength of her personality, spoke to him on a visceral level. He briefly entertained the thought of always having her welcoming him home, then pushed the ridiculous notion aside. She'd made abundantly clear her dislike for Montana. And the fact that she had no intention of staying.

Unlike Jessica, Fiona showed no signs of strain. His defiant grandmother wasn't about to let shots fired into her home rattle her. She motioned Ross to his seat and called for Chang Soo to bring him a plate. Ross had to admit that, in spite of his frustration, he was hungry. He also noted that neither Jessica nor his grandmother had done more than play with the food on their plates.

"Did you find anything?" Jessica asked.

He wished he could say something concrete to reassure her. "I found where the shot was fired."

"From the road?" Fiona asked.

Jessica's pretty face puckered in a frown. "The highway's five miles away. Can a bullet travel that far?"

Ross shook his head. "The main gate is five miles, but there's a secondary road that curves within a couple hundred yards of the house on the southeast side. Apparently, someone stopped there long enough to shoot, then took off."

Jessica's demeanor lightened. "Then you found evidence? Tire tracks? Footprints?"

"The weather's warming fast," Ross said, "and the sun had melted all but the most blurred outlines. There was nothing we could use."

"Not even a shell casing?" The indomitable Fiona allowed her disappointment to show momentarily.

"Nothing," Ross said. "A technician is still searching with a metal detector, but my gut tells me the shooter retrieved the empty cartridge."

"No luck from the dragnet?" Jessica asked.

"From all reports," Ross said, "the roads are empty this morning."

"He couldn't disappear into thin air," Jessica insisted.

"Although the population is small," Ross explained, "Swenson is a big county geographically. It took a while to put the dragnet in place. If the shooter is familiar with the county, he could have found a place to hide and lay low until the dragnet's lifted."

Chang Soo set a plate in front of him, and Ross dug into his breakfast.

Jessica placed her napkin on the table and stood. "If you'll excuse me, I need to make a phone call."

"You can use the phone in my office," Ross said.

"Thanks." She hurried from the room, her limp even more noticeable than it had been before he'd thrown her to the floor after the shooting, and he felt a pang of guilt, hoping he hadn't exacerbated her injuries.

The memory of that contact made his blood sing. Already pumped with adrenaline, he'd found himself intoxicated by the scent of her, the exotic fragrance of her hair and the subtle feminine essence that was uniquely her own. Her small body had felt deliciously right beneath his, and he'd been overwhelmed not only by the urge to protect her but also the desire to hold her in his arms....

"Ross," Fiona was saying. "Have you heard anything I've said?"

"Sorry," Ross said. "Must have been thinking about the case."

"You'd better check on Jessica."

"The shooter's not within miles of here now. Jessica's perfectly safe in my office."

"It's not her safety that concerns me at the moment." His grandmother's voice had turned frosty.

"What's up?"

"I think Jessica's leaving."

"Can you blame her? She probably feels about as comfortable here as a pig at a barbecue." He squelched his own feelings of disappointment and eyed his grandmother curiously. "Won't Max just send someone else? Or come himself?"

Fiona gave a dignified sniff. "And have the new person terrorized as well? Besides, I *like* her. I can say for a fact that Max won't come, and who knows how I'll feel about Jessica's replacement?"

Ross studied his grandmother with interest. Her petulance was totally out of character. The tragic events of the past year must have taken an even greater toll than he'd realized. He pushed away from the table, went to her and placed his arm around her shoulders.

"What do you want me to do?" he asked gently.

"See that Jessica stays until the job's done. Maybe you'll have caught the killer by then."

"I can't guard her every minute," he reminded her.

"I have no doubt you'll keep her safe," Fiona said in her don't-argue-with-me tone.

"Like I kept Kathy safe?" Pain filled his heart.

"You didn't know there was a threat then. Now you do." Fiona patted his hand. "Now go. See what our guest is up to."

He planted a kiss on her thick white hair and left the room.

JESSICA PIROUETTED before the cheval mirror in the guest room. She had learned early in her career that business assignments often included being wined and dined by clients, so luckily she'd planned accordingly. Her red silk dress, barely covering her shoulders and floating well above her knees, would be perfect for a holiday open house in Miami. For this one in Montana, however, she expected to freeze to death.

She had tried to think of an excuse to avoid this evening's party, but Fiona had been unbending.

"You need some fun after what you've been through yesterday and this morning," her hostess had insisted.

"I can take care of Courtney for you," Jessica had offered, which only proved the depth of her desperation to avoid going out into the freezing night.

"Buck Bender, our foreman, and his wife, Alma, are having Courtney sleep over," Fiona had said, "so you're free to enjoy yourself."

"I could make a good dent organizing Ross's office while you're gone," Jessica said.

"That can wait another day," Fiona said reasonably. "It's waited this long."

"But I won't know anyone at the party."

"Nonsense. You know Ross and me. And John Hayes, whom you met at the bank. Our hosts, Judge Chandler and his wife, Julie, are lovely people. They make all guests who enter their home feel as if they're old friends."

Arguing with Fiona had given her a headache, and Jessica had finally given in. She hadn't, however, lost her earlier argument with Ross. He'd entered his office just as she'd finished her phone call.

"I have a flight booked out of Billings tomorrow night at eight," she told him. "If someone here can't take me to the airport, I'll arrange for a limo or rental car."

He'd merely nodded, and his lack of reaction disappointed her. Somehow she'd hoped he'd try to make her stay. Anger at herself kicked in at the thought. Why should she care whether he liked having her around?

Because you're beginning to like having him around, an inner voice taunted her.

All the more reason to leave, she assured herself.

"You're right," he said. "You'll be much safer in Miami."

His statement made her laugh. "Most folks don't think of Miami as particularly safe."

"No?" He seemed surprised.

"There's the old story about a man who'd been transferred to Miami and went to look for a house before moving his family," she said. "Have you heard it?"

Ross shook his head and settled into one of the deep leather chairs. "Tell me."

Jessica perched on the arm of the chair opposite him. "The man went into a bar for a drink and was lamenting to the man beside him what a high-crime area he'd heard Miami was. The bar patron, a native, laughed at the newcomer's fears. 'Why, Miami's one of the safest cities in America. I've lived here all my life.' His assurances made the newcomer feel better.

The newcomer sipped his drink and decided to make his first friend in his new city. 'What do you do for a living?' he asked the bar patron. 'I'm a tailgunner on a bread truck,' the man replied.''

Ross laughed, as she'd hoped he would, and she enjoyed the richness of his voice and the temporary absence of the tension that had gripped him since the morning's shooting.

''And you still believe you'll be safer in Miami than here?'' he asked.

''No one's after me in Miami.''

His expression sobered. ''Are you sure?''

''Why would they be?''

He leaned forward, clasping his big hands between his knees and fixing her with a stare that made her want to squirm under its intensity. ''You were the unmistakable mark of the pickup that sideswiped you.''

''Road rage, you said yesterday.'' She didn't like the turn the conversation had taken. She'd made enemies in her business, but surely none who'd stoop to murder. ''Whoever had been on that deserted stretch of highway at that particular time would have been the victim.''

''Maybe.'' His voice remained calm, reasonable, soothing, a sound she thought she'd never tire of. ''But you clearly were the intended target in the solarium this morning.''

''Fiona said the shot might have been intended to

terrorize, not to kill. Why would anyone want to terrorize me?''

Ross's expression was somber. ''Had you not moved your head in the second the shot was fired, you'd be dead now. CSU worked out the trajectory. There's no doubt where the shooter was aiming.''

Jessica couldn't believe it. Someone had it out for the McGarretts, not her. If she'd been the target, her death would have served to terrorize them. The attempt hadn't been personal. Not that she would have been any less dead if the shooter had been successful.

''All the more reason for me to go home,'' she said. ''If my association with the McGarretts is making me vulnerable, the more distance I place between the Shooting Star Ranch and myself, the safer I'll feel.''

''Your association with us might explain this morning's shooting,'' Ross said. ''But what about yesterday's attack on your car? Nobody but John Hayes, Fiona and I knew that you were headed to Shooting Star Ranch.''

''Coincidence,'' Jessica said.

''I don't believe in coincidence,'' Ross said.

''Then maybe Hayes said something to someone about my assignment here.''

''John's always discreet, especially where bank business is concerned.''

''And Fiona?''

Ross smiled, a move that lit his remarkable brown

eyes and lifted his lips in a heart-stopping expression. "My grandmother doesn't approve of gossip."

"And you?"

Ross shrugged. "Didn't know who you were until you handed me your card in Hayes's office. I was a little busy after that."

Jessica shook her head. "I know you're anxious to have your estate settled—"

"I'm anxious to keep you from harm."

The look in his eyes and the determination in his voice had sent a thrill down her spine, one she instantly quashed. Even if she was looking for a man in her life—which she wasn't—Ross McGarrett would be the last person on earth she'd choose. He was too big, too dangerous, too disorganized and too settled in Montana.

The smartest thing Jessica could do was make tracks for Miami and leave the McGarrett Trust assignment to someone else. After all that had happened to her, surely Max wouldn't object to her refusal to finish the job.

As she fastened the long, dangling gold earrings that set off the highlights in her hair, she steeled herself for a night with strangers and found comfort in the thought that this time tomorrow she'd be on her way home.

A knock sounded at the guest-room door, and she answered it to find Ross standing there, his arms piled with furs.

"Fiona sent these," he explained.

Curious, Jessica stepped aside and motioned him into the room. He was dressed for the party, looking irresistibly attractive in a black cashmere turtleneck, dark slacks and a camel-colored sports jacket. He wore boots, but these were highly polished with silver inserts that matched the buckle on his belt.

As striking a man as she'd ever laid eyes on, she had to admit, and at the flutter in her heart at the sight of him, she was glad she was leaving tomorrow. She'd promised herself never to become emotionally entangled with a man, in order to avoid the heartbreak she'd witnessed in her parents. If she remained at the Shooting Star much longer, Ross would be a hard man to ignore.

Apparently unaware of the reaction he generated in her, he carried his bundle to the bed, dropped it there, then picked up one of the pieces and shook it out. It was a long coat of luxuriant, thick sable.

"We can't have you freezing to death." He held the coat open. "Try it on."

"I can't wear your grandmother's coat," Jessica protested.

"Why not?"

"What will she wear?"

Ross laughed. "Fiona has half a dozen of these. She's happy to lend you this one."

Unable to resist, Jessica slipped her arms into the satin lining of the fur and tugged the coat around her. The soft fur of the high collar brushed her cheeks, and the hem fell just above her ankles. Head to toe, she was enveloped in delicious warmth.

Ross stepped back and surveyed her with an admiring glance. "Looks good."

"As long as I don't run into any animal rights activists," Jessica said with a rueful smile.

"Fiona's had that coat since before I was born. No one loves animals more than she does, but she's a pragmatist. She says not wearing the coat won't bring the little creatures back to life, and every time she puts it on, she's grateful to them for the warmth they've provided."

Jessica ran her hands along the silky texture. "It is lovely."

"Lovely," Ross agreed with a strange hitch in his voice. "There's a hat," he added quickly, "and fur-lined boots. Put them on, and I'll meet you downstairs. Fiona is almost ready."

Ross left, and Jessica slipped on the boots, styled to wear over high-heeled shoes. Although Fiona was taller, her feet weren't that much bigger than Jessica's, so the boots were a comfortable fit.

She adjusted the fur hat at a jaunty angle and decided that she might survive the evening without turning into a block of ice after all.

If someone didn't shoot at her again.

WITH CONFLICTING EMOTIONS, Ross watched Jessica descend the stairs. A beautiful woman in her own right, she was even more striking in the elegant sable coat and hat, a creature any man would be proud to escort.

She was also in terrible danger.

And what the hell was he supposed to do about it? His gut, usually an extremely reliable indicator where fighting crime was concerned, had suddenly gone haywire on him. One minute he was certain the attacks on Jessica were merely fallout related to the militant group's vendetta against his family.

Then, when he considered that since Kathy's death, no attempts or even threats had been made against the McGarretts, he had to wonder whether someone was specifically out to harm Jessica Landon. And if so, why?

He wished she'd reconsider her decision to leave. If someone was after her, she'd be far safer at the Shooting Star than in the crowded city of Miami, where anyone could strike out of nowhere and disappear in an instant.

Isn't that what happened here this morning? he reminded himself.

He rationalized, however, that the Shooting Star had a first-rate security system, and that Chang Soo, his foreman, Buck Bender, and his crew, and Ross himself would be on constant alert. If Jessica didn't leave the ranch without an escort, he could keep her safe until he figured out where the threat was coming from.

Who was he kidding? he thought with frustration as he held the front door open for his grandmother and Jessica to exit. It had been over a year, and he was no closer to finding Kathy's killer than he had been the day of her death.

He hurried the women into the car to lessen the time they'd serve as targets in the brilliant moonlight gleaming on the thick snowfall. If he was honest with himself, he had to admit Jessica was no safer with him than in Miami.

Then why did he want her to stay?

He realized with a start that, more than anything, he wanted to know her better. She had struck a chord in him ever since their first encounter in the bank, making him experience emotions he'd never known existed. Emotions not even Kathy had stirred.

And what good would knowing more about Jessica do him? Squat squared. She obviously couldn't leave Montana fast enough.

With a sigh, he turned his thoughts from the woman in the passenger seat to the string of unsolved crimes that haunted him. As much as he disliked social functions, he was looking forward to the Chandlers' open house. Practically everyone in the county had been invited, and, with the liquor flowing freely, people would be less likely to guard their words and facial expressions. Ross planned to spend the night listening and observing, hoping to spot someone in the crowd disgruntled enough to take out his frustrations on his neighbors.

The drive into town was peaceful and uneventful. Jessica and Fiona had little to say, both watching the winter landscape glide by and listening to Christmas carols on the radio. When they reached town, the streets near the Chandler house were filled with cars, and Ross had to circle the block twice before finding a parking place.

As he pulled into a recently vacated spot, his headlights speared a man climbing out of the car in front of them. Short and squat with thick dark eyebrows and narrowed eyes visible beneath his hat, the man was a stranger, no one Ross had ever seen before.

Beside him, Jessica gasped.

In the light from the dashboard, he saw that her gaze was riveted on the stranger and all the color had drained from her face.

"Something wrong?" Ross asked.

"It can't be," Jessica murmured.

Fiona leaned forward between the seats, looking first to Jessica, then to the stranger who was walking past their car toward the Chandlers' front entrance.

"Who's that?" his grandmother asked.

"Never saw him before," Ross answered.

"I have," Jessica said in a strangled tone. "In a Chicago courtroom. He threatened to kill me."

Chapter Six

"He threatened to kill you?" Ross's words exploded in the confines of the car. "You told me no one had a grudge against you!"

"No one in Swenson County," Jessica corrected him hotly. "How was I supposed to know he'd show up here? I thought he was serving time in a federal prison in Illinois."

Fiona withdrew into the back seat. "I'll go on inside," she said diplomatically, "and let you two sort this out."

Before Ross could reply, his grandmother had climbed from the car and closed the door. He killed the engine and turned to Jessica. By the flare of his nostrils and the glint in his eyes, she could tell he was angry.

"Who is he?" Ross asked.

"Dixon Traxler."

"Is that name supposed to mean something?"

His question surprised her. "You've never heard of him?"

"We don't hear of a lot of people in this part of the world," Ross said irritably. "How about filling me in."

Jessica couldn't believe anyone with a television hadn't heard of Traxler. Several years ago, she couldn't turn on a network or cable news show without seeing his snarling face. Then she recalled there hadn't been a TV in Ross's office or living room. With running the ranch and serving as sheriff, he probably had no time for viewing.

"Dixon Traxler was CEO of Traxler-Hartman," she explained, "the accounting firm for Q-Tonics."

Recognition dawned on Ross's face, chasing away his angry look. "The huge electronics outfit that went bust several years ago. I remember that."

"It was the first in a string of corporate scandals," Jessica said. "Their executives, with help from Traxler-Hartman accountants, cooked the books, leaving their shareholders high and dry and their employees pensionless."

"What's Traxler doing here?"

His question sent a chill down Jessica's spine that even Fiona's sable couldn't quell. "Last I heard of him," she answered, "he was sentenced to one of those cushy, country club–style federal prisons—after paying several million dollars in fines."

"Why did he threaten to kill you?" Ross demanded.

Jessica lifted her chin and met his gaze head-on. "Because Max Rinehart and Associates were instrumental in blowing the whistle on Traxler-Hartman. We were called in by the board of Q-Tonics to evaluate the company's financial health. Max put me in charge, my first major assignment.''

''And you uncovered the fraud?''

Jessica laughed sharply. ''Uncovered isn't the right word. More like stepped into it ankle deep. Traxler was so greedy, he wasn't careful. Any Girl Scout could have followed his paper trail.''

''So what's he doing in Swenson County?'' Ross asked again.

''Maybe he was released early on good behavior. As for his being here, maybe that's coincidence.''

Ross shook his head, his expression fierce. ''I'm not buying that. You say he threatened you?''

Remembering the venom in Traxler's warning all those years ago, Jessica shivered. ''He was an equal-opportunity intimidator. He threatened everyone. Even the media. After being caught and convicted, he was mad at the world.''

Ross squinted through the icy windshield at the vehicle Traxler had driven. ''Is that the car that drove you off the road?''

Jessica followed his gaze. ''It's an SUV, not a pickup. And the windows aren't tinted.''

''Traxler could have switched cars.'' Ross pulled a notebook from his pocket and scribbled the license-plate number. ''I'll have my deputies check with dealers and rental companies in the area. See if anyone turned in or traded a damaged truck.''

"Look," Jessica explained, "Dixon Traxler gives me the willies and is as mean as they come. He didn't hesitate to rob folks blind, people who needed their money to live on. But I don't think he'd attempt murder."

Ross cocked an eyebrow. "Why not?"

"He's too big a coward. And he never gets his hands dirty. At Q-Tonics, his underlings did the stealing—at his direction, of course."

"So he could hire someone to do his killing for him?" Ross's voice was as cold as the rapidly dropping temperature in the car.

His implication jolted Jessica. "I hadn't thought of that. Even after paying his fines and court costs, I'm sure the man has millions socked away."

"Unfortunately, it doesn't take millions to hire a killer," Ross said between gritted teeth. "Just the luck to find someone greedy and evil enough to do the job."

Jessica didn't know if she was trembling from the cold or the subject. "So what do we do?"

Ross must have noticed her discomfort. "First we get you inside where it's warm. Then we find out what Traxler's doing in this corner of Montana."

He slid from the car, circled it and opened her door. Jessica hopped out, glad for the protection of Fiona's furs. Ross took her hand and tucked it beneath his arm. "Don't want you to slip on the ice," he explained.

His concern warmed her, even in the subarctic

windchill, but his caution was unnecessary. The side-walks were clear, apparently salted and sanded by the Chandlers for the arrival of their guests, but Jessica didn't draw away. Her glimpse of Dixon Traxler, on top of everything else that had happened since her arrival in Montana, left her shaken. Her closeness to Ross was a comfort and made her feel safe.

For the moment.

INSIDE THE BRIGHTLY LIGHTED FOYER of the Chandler home, the sounds and smells of the holidays greeted arriving guests. Ross took a deep breath of air fragrant with freshly cut evergreens, bayberry candles and a melange of spices. A sound system, barely audible above the babble of voices emanating from the great room, played Bing Crosby's ''White Christmas.''

But the familiar holiday atmosphere brought him no happiness. Already frustrated by the fact that Kathy's murder had gone too long unsolved, he worried now whether another individual with homicidal intent had entered his district, or whether his old nemesis had reared his ugly head. Ross's days wouldn't be merry or bright, the crooning Crosby notwithstanding, until he'd solved the rash of crimes that plagued Swenson County. As in any homicide investigation, until the perp was caught, everyone was a suspect. Even his friends. That thought gave him no pleasure, but only strengthened his resolve.

A maid, dressed in black with a crisp white apron,

took their coats and helped Jessica tug off her boots. Ross watched as Jessica, mouthwateringly sexy in her stunning red dress and strappy heels, shed her sable, and he was momentarily distracted. Every man in the house would envy him when he walked in with her.

Reluctantly, he forced his attention from the creamy smoothness of her bare shoulders and the delectable turn of her slim ankles and reminded himself of his duty. He had a killer to catch. And perhaps another would-be murderer as well.

Jessica leaned toward him. "What if we find that Traxler has a perfectly innocent reason to be in Swenson?" she asked softly, as if she'd been following his thoughts.

"I'll still have my deputies check his every move for the last two days," Ross said.

A tiny frown creased the skin between her feathery eyebrows. "You're serious?"

"Attempted murder does that to me."

"But it's not Traxler's style."

Ross thought for a moment. "I'll also have my homicide detectives contact others involved in Traxler's trial—the attorneys, the judge, jury members— to see if attempts have been made to harm any of them."

Her magnificent blue eyes widened in alarm. "You don't think Max might be in danger? He's like a father to me." She bit her lip nervously. "If anything happened to him…"

"We'll put him on alert, just in case."

Ross felt an irresistible urge to pull her into his arms, right there in front of God and half of Swenson County, and to swear to keep her safe, but he forced himself to keep his distance. If the morning's shooter hadn't been Traxler, but someone out to get at the McGarretts, the last impression Ross wanted to give was that Jessica was anything more than a houseguest. After all, that's all she was.

Yeah, right. Then why is your brain racing, trying to think of ways to keep her from leaving tomorrow? his conscience demanded.

I'm just trying to keep her safe, in case Traxler's a threat, he argued with himself.

"Ross, glad you could make it!" Judge Harry Chandler's booming voice interrupted Ross's inner debate. "Your department's been so busy lately, I was afraid you couldn't come."

"Hello, Harry. You know I wouldn't miss your annual bash. This is Jessica Landon, our houseguest."

With impressive ease and graciousness, Jessica offered their host her hand. "Thank you for including me tonight."

Chandler, who looked more like a cattle driver than a judge with his weather-beaten face, ruddy cheeks, thinning red hair and bowlegged build, beamed at Jessica with obvious appreciation. "Glad to have you, little lady. Fiona's told us all about you. Julie!" he boomed across the room to his wife.

"Come over here. There's somebody I want you to meet."

Julie Chandler, tall, dark, rake thin and elegantly stylish in a long black, beaded dress, the antithesis of her homespun husband, threaded her way through the crowd. Strange bedfellows, Ross always thought, every time he saw the pair together. Julie was as polished as her husband was rough-hewn, but every bit as friendly.

"Welcome to Swenson." The judge's wife extended her hand to Jessica when her husband introduced them "You must have lunch with me while you're here."

"Thanks, but I'm leaving tomorrow," Jessica said.

Chandler's bushy eyebrows shot upward. "So soon?"

"Miss Landon's from Miami," Fiona, who'd just joined them, said quickly. "The cold is too much for her."

The judge scratched his chin. "I can understand that. Winters here take getting used to. Just glad to hear you weren't scared away by that stray shot this morning."

It was Jessica's turn to look surprised.

"Not much gets by the judge," Ross explained. "He keeps a scanner radio in his study. Monitors my department and the state patrol."

"Come with me." Julie took Jessica's arm. "Let me introduce you to everyone. You don't mind, do you, Ross?"

Ross was surprised to find that he did. The time he'd have to spend with Jessica was ticking away. He couldn't kid himself by insisting he wanted to stay close to protect her. In the middle of the crowd in the Chandlers' home, she was probably as safe as she'd be anywhere.

"Enjoy yourself," Ross said to Jessica. "And don't forget to sample the stuffed mushrooms. They're Julie's specialty."

His grandmother and Jessica accompanied Julie into the crowd, and Ross turned to the judge. "Hate to take you away from your party, but I need a minute alone."

Chandler's expression sobered. "Let's move into my study."

Ross followed the judge down the hall into a mahogany-paneled room, its walls lined with shelves filled with law books. The aroma of pipe tobacco hung in the air.

Chandler closed the door behind them, blocking out the hubbub from the party rooms, and turned to Ross. "What's up?"

"Dixon Traxler."

"What about him?"

"What's he doing here?"

"I invited him."

"Why?"

Chandler bristled. "Since when do I have to vet my guest list with the sheriff?"

"Since one of your guests made a death threat against a guest of mine."

Chandler's irritation turned to puzzlement. "What the hell are you talking about?"

"Jessica Landon." Ross struggled to remain objective. Just the sound of her name on his lips made his thoughts wander to the effect she had on him. "Her firm blew the whistle on Traxler-Hartman. Traxler swore he'd make her pay. She comes to town, two attempts are made against her life, and then I find out Traxler's here, too. I don't believe in coincidence."

"You've got it all wrong." Chandler broke into a smile, waved Ross into a seat and took the chair opposite him. "Dixon was my college roommate. I invited him here months ago. He enjoys hunting, and so do I."

Ross wondered just what kind of prey Traxler had in mind. "He bring his own gun?"

"You know he can't own a gun," Chandler said. "He's a convicted felon. I've loaned him one of mine."

"A .223 caliber with a scope, by any chance?"

"Now, look here—"

"What will your constituents think," Ross demanded, "of you fraternizing with an ex-con?"

Chandler shook his head. "You really need to stay in better touch with the rest of the world, Ross."

"What's that supposed to mean?"

"Traxler's prison experience has been all over the national news."

"Prison experience?"

"Dixon found religion while he was serving his time," the judge explained. "Started a prison ministry. Even wrote a book. It hit the stores last week and is already a bestseller."

"You believe him?" Ross knew too many sociopaths who had faked conversions from a life of crime. He had to view Traxler with a healthy dose of skepticism.

"He's paid his debt to society," Chandler said. "And he's shown remorse."

"Mind loaning me the gun he's been using?" Ross asked.

"Got a warrant for it?"

Ross grimaced. "You know damn well I don't, since you're the one who'd have to issue it."

"I don't want to embarrass my guest."

"Then don't tell him. Just slip me the gun. I'll have it checked quickly and give it back to you."

Chandler heaved to his feet. "All right. Have one of your deputies pick it up tomorrow."

"Where was Traxler this morning?"

Chandler shrugged. "Sleeping in, probably. He's been staying at the hotel. Didn't want to get in the way of Julie's party preparations. He's a thoughtful guy."

Maybe too thoughtful, Ross mused. Prison gave a man plenty of time to ponder, to plot his revenge.

On the other hand, maybe Traxler *had* found religion behind bars. Stranger things had happened. Ross wasn't cutting Traxler any slack, however, until his investigation proved the man was clean.

In the meantime, he wanted to keep Jessica close and out of Traxler's reach. To do that, he'd have to convince her not to return to Miami until his inquiries had ruled Traxler either in or out.

And what will you use as an excuse to keep her here after that? an inner voice prodded him.

Ross thrust the question away. For now, he had to deal with one problem at a time.

JESSICA CAUGHT SIGHT of Ross immediately when he and Judge Chandler returned. In a room filled with tall men, Ross towered above the others. His gaze sought hers, but she couldn't decipher the look he gave her. He left the judge, who hurried into the foyer to greet new arrivals, and worked his way through the crowd toward her.

"Have you met everyone?" he asked when he joined her and Julie.

Jessica nodded. "But please don't ask me to repeat names. My head's still spinning from so many new faces."

"If you'll excuse me," Julie said, "I should refill the punch bowl." Their hostess headed toward the kitchen.

"Where's Fiona?" Ross asked.

Jessica nodded toward a corner beside the huge

fireplace of mountain stone dominating the far wall of the room. "Who's she talking to? That's one person I didn't meet."

"Carson Kingsley. He owns the ranch south of ours. I'm surprised he's here. He usually avoids social gatherings."

"He doesn't look very happy."

"Carson's had a tough time. His wife died several years ago. He took it hard. Still does."

Jessica studied Ross. He, too, had lost a wife, and she couldn't help wondering how deeply he still grieved. Although the depth of his grief was none of her concern, she reminded herself. After all, she was leaving tomorrow and would never lay eyes on Ross McGarrett again.

The realization made her unexpectedly sad, but she chalked up the feeling to the incessant Christmas music playing in the background. The holidays always made her unhappy. She'd be glad to return to Miami where she could avoid the sentiments of the season by holing up in her condo until the annual insanity passed.

"You can't leave tomorrow," Ross said suddenly.

Jessica viewed him with alarm. "Another blizzard? Please don't tell me the flights will be grounded."

Ross shook his head and nodded across the room toward Dixon Traxler, surrounded by a crowd of obvious admirers. "Haven't heard the weather report, but there're other reports I want to check before you head out on your own.''

As if aware of their scrutiny, Traxler looked their way and started across the room toward them. Jessica could feel Ross stiffen beside her. She didn't relish facing her old adversary and was glad for Ross's comforting presence as Traxler descended on them.

''Jessica Landon,'' Traxler said with unexpected warmth, reaching for her hand. ''What a surprise! What are you doing in Montana?''

Suppressing her revulsion, Jessica allowed him to grasp her fingers, but only briefly. ''I might ask you the same thing.''

''Visiting old friends,'' Traxler said. ''Your being here, too, is serendipitous. I've been meaning to look you up.''

''To carry out your threat?'' The words slipped out before Jessica could bite them back.

Traxler looked stunned. ''To apologize. I deserved my punishment and more. At the time, I wanted to shift the blame to you. But I've finally admitted that if I hadn't committed the crime, you wouldn't have caught me.''

Surprise left her tongue-tied. Ross stepped in to fill the conversation gap. ''Noble sentiments,'' he commented, his rich voice heavy with irony.

''And absolutely sincere,'' Traxler insisted. ''I'm a changed man. I have something for you, Jessica. Wait here. I'll be right back.''

"Do you believe him?" Ross asked when Traxler was out of earshot.

"As much as I believe in Santa Claus," Jessica said. "But changed or not, he still gives me the creeps."

Before she could say more, Traxler was back, holding an object toward her. "This is for you."

Jessica reached for it, but Ross intercepted it.

"It's only a book," Traxler said with a bit of a whine.

Ross handled the volume gingerly, as if expecting it to explode. His actions informed Jessica that the sheriff didn't trust Traxler, either. Once Ross had flipped through the pages and apparently convinced himself the book was harmless, he gave it to her.

Dixon Traxler's smiling face stared back at her from the cover. The title, *A New Man, A New Life*, was emblazoned in brilliant white across the royal-blue dust jacket.

"I hear it's a bestseller," Ross said.

Traxler beamed. "It's doing quite well."

"And since you've changed so much—" Jessica forced her sweetest smile "—I'm sure you'll use the profits to reimburse all those poor people you swindled."

Traxler's previous benevolent air evaporated like mist in strong sunlight. "I worked hard to write this book. Blood, sweat and tears. I deserve the profits."

Jessica's anger skyrocketed. "The employees of Q-Tonics worked hard for their pensions, too."

Suddenly Ross's hand was gripping her elbow, so tightly it was almost painful. "Fiona's signaling us to join her. If you'll excuse us, Traxler?"

Without waiting for Jessica's consent, Ross propelled her across the floor toward the corner where Fiona sat with Carson Kingsley.

"I've known it from the moment I first saw you," Ross whispered in her ear in a low, fierce voice.

"Known what?" Jessica demanded, trying without success to extricate herself from his grip.

"That you have a death wish."

"You're right," Jessica said irritably. "That's why I agreed to come to Montana in December."

"You know what I'm talking about." Ross almost hissed in her ear. "If Traxler's out to kill you, why give him more reason?"

"How much reason does he need? I'd think putting him in prison is reason enough."

"Then insulting him will only make him more determined," Ross said.

"He's either made up his mind to kill me or he hasn't," Jessica said. "Being polite at this stage won't make a difference."

They passed the fireplace, and she took immense satisfaction in throwing *A New Man, A New Life* into the roaring blaze.

Fiona looked up and frowned as they approached. Jessica guessed the older woman must have sensed the tension between them.

"Having a good time?" Fiona asked, as if expecting a negative response.

"It's a lovely party," Jessica assured her. "And I really like Julie. If I were staying longer, I'd like to know her better."

"Hello, Carson," Ross said. "This is Jessica Landon, our houseguest."

The middle-aged man, polite but reserved, stood to shake her hand. Jessica could sense the pain behind his pale blue eyes, reminding her that emotional involvement inevitably led to unhappiness.

"How are you liking Montana?" Carson asked in a flat, impersonal tone.

Jessica floundered for something positive to say. "Almost everyone has been very welcoming."

"Almost?" His pale eyes glinted with a strange light.

Laughter? Jessica wondered.

"Well," she hurried to correct her gaffe, "I haven't met everyone."

"This is hostile country," Carson said.

"Now, Carson," Fiona chided him gently, "it has its good points."

Carson shrugged and nodded toward Jessica. "Does she know what happened in this room?"

"This is a party," Ross said quickly. "Let's not bring up bad memories."

"You caught the man yet?" Carson asked.

Jessica took pity at the discomfort on Ross's face

and changed the subject. "Tell me about your ranch, Mr. Kingsley."

What seemed hours later, Jessica escaped, after hearing more about the feeding habits of cattle than she'd ever wanted to learn. If she hadn't known better, she'd have thought the older man was toying with her, making her uncomfortable on purpose.

"He's just lonely," Fiona insisted when Jessica joined her again. "Since his wife died, he hasn't had anyone to talk to. He keeps to himself too much. I've invited him to the Shooting Star, but he always has some excuse. This is the first time I've seen him among other people in ages. His coming here tonight is a good sign. Maybe his grief is finally beginning to heal."

For the remainder of the evening, Jessica spoke with almost every guest, avoiding only Dixon Traxler and having her ear bent again by Carson Kingsley.

Even as she was conversing with others, she was intensely aware of Ross as he worked the room. A casual observer might have thought him merely sociable, but in her business, Jessica had learned to read the nuances of conversation, knowing the closing of a deal or revelation of a client's intent could hang on a word or an inflection.

Expressing interest in his friends' and neighbors' activities, Ross was cleverly gathering information, finding who had been where both yesterday when her car had been forced off the road and this morning when the shot was fired. Not one of them appeared aware that he or she had been successfully interrogated when Ross finally moved away.

Only one conversation had hit a sour note. Jack Randall, Ross's neighbor to the north, had confronted him at the punch bowl where Ross and Jessica had gone to refill their eggnog cups.

"I'm still waiting," Randall said, anger barely hidden behind a pasted-on smile.

"Sorry, Jack," Ross said easily, "but you'll have to wait a while longer. I've been busy lately."

"Dammit," Randall almost shouted, then lowered his voice, "you're always busy. You're avoiding me on purpose."

Ross shook his head. "I'm having to deal with life-and-death matters—"

"This is a life-and-death matter to me!"

Jessica didn't have to be a trained observer to sense that Randall's frustration had reached the boiling point.

"Look, Jack," Ross said in a consoling tone, "I'm willing to examine the old survey you've found, but it won't make a hill of beans worth of difference what I think. The boundaries registered at the courthouse are the legal ones. We both have to abide by them."

Randall, a tall, lanky man with dark hair gone gray at the temples, set his mouth in a thin, tight line. "That's easy for you to say, since those boundaries work in your favor. There's over a hundred acres in question here."

For the first time since she'd met him, Jessica saw Ross teeter on the edge of losing control, but he took a deep breath and capped his anger. "Tell you what, Jack. We'll let the lawyers sort it out. They know more about these things than either of us."

Randall's eyes blazed. "Yeah, let the McGarrett money buy your way out of this one."

Before Ross could reply, Randall turned on his heel and stomped out of the room.

Ross appeared suddenly tired, and Jessica felt sorry for him. He had enough problems as sheriff. He didn't need a turf battle with his neighbor, too.

"Why's he so angry?" she asked.

"Jack's found an old survey, one that shifts the boundary between our ranches, but since it was never registered, the document has no validity."

Jessica frowned. "A hundred acres is a lot of land."

"Not out here," Ross said with a smile. "It's what's on the land that Jack is interested in."

"Oil?" That commodity would definitely figure prominently in the estimated worth of the Shooting Star Ranch. She'd momentarily forgotten her decision to abandon her financial assessment of the McGarrett estate.

Ross laughed and the tension in him seemed to melt away. "Not oil. Something even more valuable."

Jessica's eyes widened. "Gold?"

"Water."

"Water? More valuable than gold? You're kidding."

"A creek runs through those acres Jack would like to claim as his. And cattle always need water."

"You think he's lying about the survey?" Jessica asked.

"No, Jack's an honest guy. But he doesn't want to admit the survey's worthless unless it's been registered." Ross's brown eyes softened as he gazed at her. "How are you holding up?"

Her high-heeled shoes were killing her, and she still suffered aches and pains from yesterday's accident, but Jessica wasn't about to admit to her discomfort. "Fine."

"I think I should take you home."

"You don't have to leave early on my account. Since I won't be working on your records, I can sleep in tomorrow and be rested for my flight."

His strong jaw settled in a determined angle. "We'll discuss that tomorrow."

"There's nothing to discuss."

He didn't argue, but she knew from the look in his remarkable brown eyes that the subject of her imminent departure wasn't closed.

"Let's find Fiona," he said, "and pay our respects to the Chandlers."

A SHORT TIME LATER, the trio was headed home. Jessica leaned against the seat's headrest, gazed at the snow-covered landscape, glistening in the moonlight, and realized with a start how beautiful it was. Every bit as lovely in its own stark way as the moon over Miami Beach. The wintry scene filled her with an unexpected serenity, making even the endless carols on the radio less annoying. She must be mellowing in her old age. She'd not only survived but enjoyed a holiday party, and now she was sentimentalizing over snow.

She gave herself a mental shake and remembered a question she'd been wanting to ask. "Carson Kingsley asked if I knew what had happened in the Chandlers' house."

Ross's gloved hands tightened on the steering wheel. "Don't mention it to Julie. She's only now recovering."

"Recovering from what?" Jessica asked.

"A home invasion," Fiona said. "About six months ago. Very traumatic."

"Was she injured?" Jessica recalled that Julie had appeared healthy and happy at the party.

"Not physically," Ross said. A muscle ticked in his jaw, indicating his tension. "Julie was alone in the house. Someone surprised her, overpowered her, taped her mouth, covered her head with a sack and tied her to a chair."

"Robbery?" Jessica asked.

"Intimidation," Ross said. "You saw all the expensive collectibles and antiques the Chandlers have. But only one item was stolen that day, a Lladró statue of a girl with a flock of geese. Dozens of more valuable items were left behind.''

''Maybe the robbers were frightened away before they could steal more,'' Jessica said.

Fiona made a sound of disgust. ''Not likely. Poor Julie was tied up for hours before Harry came home late that night and found her.''

Jessica looked to Ross. ''Do you suspect the Swenson County Freedom Fighters?''

''I wish I knew,'' Ross said, his frustration evident. ''Whoever it was left nothing behind, not a print or a hair or a fiber. The incident could have been part of the militia group's terrorism spree. Or it could have been a criminal's revenge. Judge Chandler has handed down hundreds of stiff sentences over the years. Someone could have struck back at him through his wife.''

''How awful,'' Jessica murmured.

''*Awful*'s the operative word,'' Ross said, ''and my department hasn't been able to do a damn thing about it.''

''You're too hard on yourself,'' Fiona said soothingly. ''You'll find this man eventually. You've always said patience pays off in criminal investigations. Don't lose yours now, son.''

''We have a few slim leads,'' Ross admitted, ''but I'd be lying if I said we're close to solving these cases.''

The weariness in his voice made Jessica want to reach out to him, but she stifled the impulse to lay her hand on his sleeve. Despite Ross's objections, this time tomorrow, she'd be halfway home, three thousand miles from Sheriff McGarrett and his troubles. Surprisingly, the prospect wasn't as pleasing as it had been earlier. Had Ross spooked her with the possibility of Traxler as a threat? Those doubts must have given birth to her sudden reluctance to leave.

Before she could contemplate her change of heart further, Ross had stopped in front of the house.

"I'll put the car in the garage," he said, "then I'm headed for bed. I'll say good-night now."

Jessica and Fiona entered the house, and Jessica started up the stairs.

"Wait," Fiona said. "Have a brandy with me before going to bed."

More tired than she'd realized, Jessica started to protest, but noting the pleading in Fiona's eyes, she relented and followed the older woman into the living room.

"I've missed having another female to talk to," Fiona said. She splashed golden liquid into two snifters and handed Jessica one.

Jessica nodded. "Ross told me about Kathy. I'm sorry."

"Kathy was a disaster, in more ways than one," Fiona said cryptically, then added hastily, "but the poor girl didn't deserve what happened to her."

Jessica waited for Fiona to elaborate on why Kathy had been a disaster, but after a few sips of fine cognac, Fiona was nodding off.

Jessica finished her drink. When Fiona still hadn't awakened, she slipped away.

Entering the darkened guest room, she flipped on the overhead light. Everything was as she'd left it.

Except one.

As deep red as a bloodstain, a long-stemmed rose lay across the white lace of her pillow. After glancing nervously around the room and into the bathroom and closet to assure herself no one was hiding there, Jessica crossed to the bed and picked up the flower.

A card was attached to the stem with a red velvet bow. The ribbon was threaded through a typed note that read: "For Jessica, from your secret Santa."

Chapter Seven

Jessica's sleepiness instantly vanished. Although her body ached with weariness, her mind raced with questions.

Who had left a rose on her pillow? And even more important, why?

As far as she knew, only four people besides herself had access to the main house—Ross, Fiona, Courtney and Chang Soo. She ruled out Courtney immediately. Writing the message and obtaining the rose were far beyond a two-year-old's abilities.

Chang Soo was also an unlikely candidate. Friendly but with an impassive Asian reserve, the old man didn't seem the type to leave secret messages. And he wouldn't have called her Jessica. To Chang Soo, using her first name so familiarly would have been a sign of disrespect. And Chang Soo was nothing if not respectful.

Fiona? Jessica shook her head. No way Fiona could have delivered the rose. The older woman hadn't been out of Jessica's sight from the moment they entered the house on their return from the Chandlers'. The rose was obviously fresh and hadn't been out of water or refrigeration long, so Fiona couldn't have placed it on the pillow before the party, either.

Jessica kicked off her shoes, wiggled her aching toes in relief and sank into a chair in front of the fireplace. Her process of elimination had narrowed down her secret Santa to one prospect.

Ross.

But her mind refused to wrap itself around that possibility. Yes, Ross had had the opportunity. He could have slipped the rose into her room after parking the car, while she and Fiona sipped brandy in the living room.

But why?

Her pulse quickened at the thought that Ross might be attracted to her, but she quickly squelched that idea, for two reasons. First, the man was too immersed in the problems of unsolved crimes to have time for romance. And, second, even if he did have time, the surreptitious approach didn't seem to fit Ross's style. Sure, he'd been covert in his interviews of the Chandlers' guests tonight, but he'd been working then, doing his job. He didn't strike her as the type to be secretive in his personal relationships.

Then again, how much did she really know about Ross McGarrett? She ticked off his attributes on her fingers. He was brave. He'd risked his life for her twice, a total stranger. He was obviously thorough and conscientious about his duty as sheriff. And he was totally, hopelessly disorganized when it came to paperwork, she thought with a grimace. She felt her expression soften as she recalled his interaction with his daughter. He was also a devoted, loving father.

But could he be her secret Santa?

Her blood ran suddenly cold as she considered a fifth potential candidate. Suppose her secret messenger wasn't some benign admirer at all, but an enemy who was toying with her? Had the person who'd run her off the road or fired the shot somehow entered the McGarrett house while they were away and left the rose and card? Was the message intended to inform her that she wasn't invulnerable? That she wasn't safe?

That thought propelled her to her bare feet and into the hall. Before she could consider what she was doing, she found herself knocking on Ross's bedroom door.

Idiot, she told herself, hoping he was asleep and hadn't heard her. *You're overreacting. Go back to your room and forget the stupid rose. Tomorrow you'll be home and it won't be an issue.*

Before she could flee back to the guest room, Ross's door swung open, and she found herself staring at the broad, muscled expanse of his bare tanned chest. He'd undressed completely except for his jeans, riding low on his lean hips. His thick brown hair was tousled, and his eyelids were heavy with fatigue. He looked wonderfully sexy, he smelled enticingly male, and she wondered how touching him would feel. The prospect made her mouth go dry.

"Something wrong?" he asked.

An emotion deep inside her flared to life, and she recognized it with dismay as white-hot desire.

"No," she managed to utter, while her brain went dead.

A slow, bone-melting smile lifted his lips and lit his eyes. "You need something?"

Oh, yes!

Needs she'd never allowed herself to admit flooded her, but fortunately her sluggish brain finally kick-started again. What was she doing here? If Ross *was* her secret Santa, she didn't want to go there. More than anything, she wanted to keep imprisoned the sleeping giant of emotions walled inside her.

And if Ross *hadn't* left the rose, it didn't matter who had. She would be gone soon.

"Just wanted to say good-night," she murmured, avoiding his eyes and suppressing the urge to fall into his arms.

To her dismay and delight, he leaned down, cupped her chin in his hand and brushed her lips with his. Electricity surged through her veins, and she pushed herself up on tiptoe to receive his kiss, wanting more.

Wanting…Ross.

Until she realized what she was doing.

Feeling more foolish than she could ever remember, she pulled away and forced herself to walk, not run, toward her room.

"Jessica."

Her name on his lips was a caress, as inflaming as the sensuous touch of his lips had been. She placed a few more feet between them for safety before she turned.

"Yes?"

"Sleep well."

In addition to her bones, she felt her heart melting, too, obstinately ignoring the signals she was sending to suppress her feelings.

"You, too." Her voice came out too soft, too seductive, expressing everything she was trying not to feel.

She turned, again resisting the urge to run to her room, and she could feel his gaze following her, boring into her back the entire length of the hallway.

When she'd closed the door behind her, she stripped off her clothes, pulled on her gown and climbed into bed. Even with the lights off, the moonlight streaming through the windows illuminated the rose, lying on the bedside table, a dark red question mark in the night.

JESSICA WAS AWARE of the brilliant sunlight streaming into the room even before she opened her eyes, but she wasn't ready to leave the soft comfort of her bed. She'd taken hours to go to sleep the night before, lying awake and staring at the ceiling until after the huge grandfather clock in the downstairs hall had struck two o'clock.

Remembering Ross's kiss.

Trying *not* to remember Ross's kiss.

What was the big deal? she'd argued with herself. She was thirty-two years old, and she'd been kissed before, longer, deeper, more explicitly.

But never like this.

The kiss had been nothing, she assured herself, and meant nothing. It had lasted mere seconds. He'd just touched his lips to hers. He hadn't even held her.

Then why can't you stop thinking about it?

She had stopped thinking about it, she lied to herself. She was thinking now about getting up.

Not that she had any reason to get out of bed. She'd given up on her assignment. Max would have to send someone else to sort out the disaster Ross called an office. Guilt tweaked her at the thought. She'd never let Max down before, but surely he'd understand her leaving the Shooting Star after all that had happened. She hadn't called to tell him her plans. She figured facing him with the facts in his office once she arrived would make him unable to talk her out of her decision.

Meanwhile, she would get some more sleep.

With her thoughts returning to Ross like a homing pigeon to its roost, she inched deeper into her pillows and pulled the covers to her chin, hoping to doze off. The almost inaudible click of her doorknob brought her instantly awake.

With her wits scattered by her encounter with Ross the previous night, she'd forgotten to lock her door.

Slowly the door began to open. No one had knocked or called out a greeting. Who would be sneaking into her room in broad daylight?

Her gaze fell on the wilted rose on her bedside table. What if Ross hadn't left it after all? Had her secret Santa returned? And with what intent?

Before she could decide whether to feign sleep or scream, a pair of wide gray eyes peeped around the bottom half of the door.

"Hi."

"Courtney!" Almost dizzy with relief, Jessica sat up in bed. "I thought you were staying with the Benders."

"They bringed me home."

Barefoot and dressed only in flannel pajamas, Courtney stepped into the room and looked around with childlike curiosity. Jessica felt a flash of annoyance at the intrusion—until she noted the little girl's shivering.

"You're freezing!" Jessica threw back the covers and opened her arms. "Climb in with me."

She didn't have to ask twice. Courtney clambered up the high side of the antique four-poster and snuggled against Jessica. She drew the covers around both of them, startled by the unexpected surge of pleasure she experienced at the child's closeness. Jessica had always felt awkward around children, but holding Courtney warmed her heart.

Maybe she *was* mellowing in her old age.

"Where's Fiona?" she asked the child.

"Sleeping."

"And your daddy?"

"Sleeping."

Ross, spread-eagle naked on his bed, eyes closed with his long, thick lashes dark against his cheeks, his hair rumpled... Jessica thrust aside that compelling image. "Then who's looking after you?"

"Chan' Soo."

"Does he know where you are?"

Courtney nodded. "He sended me."

"Why?"

"'Bout breakfast." The little girl snuggled closer and wrapped her arms around Jessica's waist. "You smell nice."

Courtney smelled good, too, sweet and fresh with a hint of talcum powder, and the embrace of her chubby arms touched a maternal chord Jessica hadn't known she possessed. "Chang Soo wants to know what I want for breakfast?"

Courtney shook her head. "You want breakfast in bed?"

The lovely decadence of the proposal appealed to Jessica. Sometimes when she'd traveled on assignments and stayed in posh hotels, she'd had room service deliver breakfast, but she hadn't indulged in that luxury in a long time. Then she recalled the exposure of the solarium and dining room and decided Chang

Soo's offer to serve her upstairs was as much cautionary as pampering.

"I'd love breakfast in bed," she said.

Courtney started to scamper down. "I go tell him."

"Wait," Jessica said, holding her back as an idea struck her. "Have you had your breakfast?"

The little girl shook her head.

"Want to eat here with me?"

"Uh-huh."

The smile Courtney threw her touched her heart, and she felt a sudden kinship with the motherless little girl. From the time Jessica was born until she was sent away to boarding school at age six, she'd had a series of nannies and caretakers, but little if any attention from her mother. Since Courtney's mom had died a year ago, Jessica doubted the girl had any memories of her. Awareness of that empty hole, where a mother's love should have been, created an instant bond between her and the girl, driving away any previous awkwardness she'd felt with the child.

"Tell Chang Soo to bring breakfast for both of us," Jessica instructed. "And to find you a robe and slippers. Then you come back here to me."

Courtney scooted off the bed and headed for the door.

"Wait," Jessica called again. "Does your daddy get a Sunday newspaper?"

Courtney nodded. "A big one."

Jessica remembered seeing an edition of the *New York Times* in the solarium yesterday. "Tell Chang Soo to put the comics with our breakfast. We can read them together."

"Okay."

The beam of anticipation that lit the little girl's face almost brought tears to Jessica's eyes. It didn't take much to please the child. Jessica forced back the knowledge that it wouldn't have taken much for her own parents to please her, either, but they'd apparently never felt the inclination.

Courtney hurried out the door, and Jessica consoled herself with the fact that Courtney, at least, had a loving father and a doting great-grandmother. But she couldn't help wondering if those two factors could adequately fill the void left by Kathy's death.

She glanced around the elegant but homey room and found a sudden reluctance to leave that day, in spite of the snow sparkling outside the window. But when she remembered the red rose and unknown Santa, she realized returning to Miami was her best option if she wanted to stay safe.

But she couldn't help wondering what would happen to the McGarretts and surprised herself by realizing how much she cared.

ROSS ROLLED OVER and surveyed his bedside clock with a groan. He'd overslept, something he hadn't done in years. No wonder, however. Jessica's sudden appearance at his bedroom door last night, alluringly seductive and yet emanating a touching vulnerability, had driven all thoughts of sleep from his mind.

Something had spooked her, but he had no idea whether it was a delayed reaction from her encounter with Traxler or simply an accumulation of the disasters that had befallen her since her arrival in Swenson County. He had to give her credit. She was one plucky woman. Most people would have hightailed it back to Miami immediately after the incident in the bank. She'd weathered two more traumas before finally throwing in the towel and admitting defeat.

But what had she wanted to tell him last night? She hadn't banged on his door at that late hour just to say good-night.

He was glad she had, even though he knew he shouldn't have kissed her. If the kiss, uncomplicated as it had been, had affected her as much as it had him, she'd probably forgotten what she'd come to tell him.

But he hadn't been able to resist. Finding her standing there, so amazingly beautiful, so incredibly desirable, had short-circuited his reasoning. He'd needed every ounce of willpower not to crush her to him before she pulled away. No woman had ever had such an effect on him—and he'd certainly never been a saint where females were concerned. But what he felt for Jessica was more than desire. He wanted to know her better, in every way.

Which was never going to happen if she left tonight.

He swung out of bed and headed for the shower. He had his work cut out for him today. In addition to moving forward with his investigations, he had to convince Jessica to remain at the Shooting Star. He wanted to keep her under watch until he had assured himself that Dixon Traxler wasn't a threat to her. The man had the means and opportunity to follow her to Miami if he had mayhem on his mind. Here, Ross hoped he could keep her safe.

Not only safe, but close.

The thought pleased him, and as hot water pulsed over his skin, he came up with an idea. His plan would keep her protected for the day and allow him to have her company all to himself, giving him ample time to plead his case for her to stay at the Shooting Star to finish her assignment.

Immensely satisfied with himself, he whistled as he strode down the upstairs hall. When he reached Jessica's door, however, the sound of a low, sultry voice, punctuated by childish giggles, grabbed his attention.

Courtney, the little devil! What was she doing in Jessica's room? He knocked on the door to find out.

"Come in," Jessica called.

Ross opened the door and caught his breath at the sight that greeted him. Jessica, her magnificent auburn hair disheveled from sleep and glinting golden in the sun slanting through the window behind her, held Courtney in her lap. The two sat in one of the deep chairs, the comic pages spread out before them.

Jessica's velour robe of French blue brought out the deep color in her eyes, the flush of roses in her cheeks, the luster of her lips.

He pulled his thoughts from kissing them again and noted that his usually shy Courtney in her pink robe and bunny slippers seemed amazingly content on Jessica's lap.

On the table beside them sat a tray with the remnants of breakfast for two.

"Hi, Daddy."

The beauty and tranquillity of the domestic scene they presented raised a lump in his throat, and he had to swallow hard to speak.

"Hi, Cupcake. Good morning, Jessica." He hoped his sudden surge of desire hadn't revealed itself in either the tone of his voice or the cut of his jeans.

"I like *Peanuts*," Courtney said with a giggle.

"You're eating peanuts for breakfast?" Ross asked in faked amazement, pretending to misunderstand.

"No, silly." His daughter shook her head, and Jessica's eyes twinkled at him above Courtney's blond curls. "Snoopy and Charlie Brown."

"There's coffee left." Jessica nodded toward a thermal carafe. "And an extra cup. And sweet rolls."

Ross hesitated only briefly, pulled one way by duty, the other by the welcoming warmth of the woman and his child. It was Sunday, he reminded himself. Not much could be accomplished until tomorrow anyway, with businesses closed and people off for the weekend. With a sigh of contentment, he settled into the chair across from Jessica and Courtney and accepted the cup Jessica handed him.

"Does Granny know you're home?" he asked his daughter.

She shook her head. "Granny's asleep."

"The Benders brought Courtney back early," he explained to Jessica. "They go to Billings every other Sunday to visit Alma's mother, and they like to get an early start."

Jessica nodded, and her gaze flicked briefly from him to the table beside her bed, then back again.

He followed her gaze, but noted nothing out of the ordinary. Maybe his presence in her bedroom was making her uneasy, although Jessica didn't strike him as the uptight, prim-and-proper type.

Courtney, always a wiggle-worm, scooted off Jessica's lap.

"Where're you going, Cupcake?" Ross asked.

"Find Granny."

"Okay, but if she's not awake, don't bother her. You come right back here."

He leaned forward, and his daughter put her arms around his neck and kissed him on the lips. She tasted of sugar and hot chocolate.

"Wuv you, Daddy." Her tiny arms tightened.

He hugged her back, reluctant to let her go. He hadn't expected to love this child so much, and now he couldn't live without her. "I love you, too, Cupcake."

She pulled back, her gray eyes teasing. "Cour'ney."

The exchange was one of their favorite games. "My Courtney Cupcake," he said.

Laughing, she ran from the room.

"I have a favor to ask," he said to Jessica as soon as Courtney was gone.

"I'm not going to be here long enough to grant a favor," she said. "I'm leaving for Billings this afternoon in time to catch my evening flight."

"That's where the favor comes in."

She cocked her head, her expression curious. "You need something taken to Billings?"

"I need you to stay."

The roses in her cheeks darkened a shade, and he realized too late the potential double meaning of his words.

"I mean, I want you to stay," he corrected, making the ambiguity even worse.

She lifted her feathery eyebrows over questioning eyes, but said nothing.

He set his cup aside, leaned forward and spread his hands. "Let me explain."

"I'm listening."

"We have a situation here—"

"We?"

"I have a situation. At least, the sheriff's department does."

He couldn't be certain, but he thought he saw a

brief flicker of disappointment cross her face before she composed it again.

"Yesterday's shooting?" she asked.

He nodded. "We don't know what we're facing. There's the possibility what's happened to you is totally unrelated to other incidents in Swenson County."

"So if I leave tonight, I'm no longer your problem," she said reasonably.

"I can't let you do that."

Her eyes widened with a hint of anger. "You can't stop me."

"Actually, that's not completely true." He tried to keep from smiling at the possible solution called to mind by her comment.

She stood, her robe swirling around her, and walked away from him, toward the window. Sunlight turned her hair to burnished gold, and his fingers itched to twine themselves in it. Turning, she confronted him, hands on her hips. She was every bit as magnificent when she was angry as she had been at his bedroom door last night.

"What are you going to do?" she insisted hotly. "Arrest me?"

"If I have to," he answered easily.

"You can't be serious! On what charges?"

"As a material witness." He rose and went to her, taking her by the shoulders and turning her until he stood between her and the window. He didn't want her making a target of herself.

"But you're a reasonable woman, so I'm hoping an arrest won't be necessary."

She was also an extremely intelligent woman and apparently realized immediately the purpose of his maneuver. "We should both stay away from the windows," she said, her voice less angry now.

He nodded and released her. She returned to her chair. Ross followed, propped his elbow on the mantel and gazed down at her. "Will you hear me out?"

"Will you slap the cuffs on me if I don't?" Her tone was serious, but he caught a glint of teasing in her eyes. Longing surged through him again, and he forced himself to take a deep breath and keep his mind on business.

"As I mentioned earlier, I don't know whether the attempts on your life are related to other incidents in the county or not. Dixon Traxler's presence here creates the distinct possibility that they're not."

She shuddered at the man's name. "I was ready to go before. Traxler's being here makes leaving an even better idea."

"If Traxler followed you here," Ross said pointedly, "he can follow you anywhere."

She shrugged. "So I alert the Miami-Dade Sheriff's Office when I return home that the man's a threat."

"And will the sheriff of Dade County invite you to stay in his home and offer to be your personal bodyguard?"

"Don't be ridiculous."

"I'm being practical. Until I can check Traxler out, you're safer here with me."

"Only if Dixon Traxler's the real threat," she said. "If someone's after Ross McGarrett and the other county officials, I'm in *more* danger with you."

"Not if we're careful," he argued, not wanting to concede her point. "Look, all I'm asking is for you to wait a few days. During that time, my detectives can check out Traxler's vehicles, run the ballistics on the rifle he borrowed from the judge—"

"What?" Her eyes widened in alarm. "You're telling me Traxler has a gun?"

"He says he came here to hunt," Ross said. "I want time to find out if he's lying."

"The man's a habitual liar," Jessica said. "I can tell you that without an investigation."

Ross had guessed as much from just meeting the man, but he needed evidence before he could make an arrest. "I also want time to see if others involved in his trial have had threats made against them—or attempts on their lives."

"You can mount your investigation whether I return to Miami or not."

He resisted the urge to go to her and run his hands through her hair, to pull her into his arms. "But I can't keep you safe if you're in Miami."

"I'm not your responsibility," she said softly.

"But you are." He'd spoken with more emotion than he'd intended. Clearing his throat, he continued in a more even tone. "You were attacked on the road in my county and as a guest in my home. That makes you my responsibility.''

He could see his arguments were swaying her, could observe her determination wavering. He waited, giving her time to decide.

''How many days will it take to clear Traxler?'' she asked.

''I can't say for certain. I'm hoping by Wednesday that we'll have some indication of his guilt or innocence. Enough to know whether it's safe for you to return to Miami.'' And by then, he hoped he'd have convinced her to stay until...

The stress of his job had to be catching up with him. He'd only met Jessica a few days before, and already he was hoping she'd stay indefinitely.

Her forehead wrinkled in a thoughtful frown. ''I suppose I could stay until Wednesday. I can spend that time in your office, arranging files and information for whoever takes my place.''

''I have a better idea,'' Ross said.

Jessica looked doubtful. ''Why do I get the feeling I'm not going to like this?''

He threw her a challenging smile. ''Because you have no sense of adventure?''

''What's that supposed to mean?''

He couldn't help goading her, pressing to gain his objective. ''I figure you fiscal types are all alike. Rather have your head stuck in ledger books or computer financial programs than out enjoying nature.''

''Enjoying nature? In that snowbound icebox?''

She jerked her head toward the window. "You must be crazy!"

"You haven't seen the summer camp," Ross said easily, "where we graze the herd in warm weather."

"It isn't summer! And the weather definitely isn't warm."

"The camp's even more beautiful in winter."

Her eyes narrowed with suspicion, as if she realized she was being set up but didn't know what to do about it. "Where is this summer camp?"

"In the mountains, about twenty miles west of here."

"Accessible by road?"

Ross shook his head. "Only by trails. We drive the cattle from horseback, or sometimes using vehicles with four-wheel drive."

She looked at him as though he'd been crazy to suggest such an outing. "Neither horses nor four-wheel drive can make it to the mountains in that snow."

"You're right," he admitted.

She appeared to relax, as if considering the subject closed.

"We'll go by snowmobile," he said.

Her tension returned instantly. "Now I know you've lost your mind."

He shook his head. "We'll be on Shooting Star land the entire trip. You can write it up for your report."

"And we'll be a prime target for anyone with a rifle."

"Not if no one except Fiona knows where we're going. We'll be so bundled up that, even if we're spotted, no one will know who we are. There shouldn't be anyone on the property this time of year anyway. It's posted against hunting. And all my hands are bunked here at the main house until spring."

"What about your job? You can't just drive away while you have crimes under investigation."

"I'll make all my calls and assignments before we leave. And I'll take along a shortwave radio to keep in touch with dispatch."

Her eyes flashed in triumph, as if she suddenly knew she'd outfoxed him. "But who's going to guard Fiona and Courtney while we're gone?"

"Chang Soo," Ross replied.

"He's an old man." She stared at Ross as though he'd grown two heads.

"And an expert in martial arts," Ross said, remembering how the old man had managed to best even Ross's most skillful deputies in hand-to-hand combat. "Besides, ever since yesterday's shooting, I've had several of the hands on rotating shifts, guarding the house and the property 24/7. I'm afraid you've run out of reasons for us not to visit the summer camp."

A smug smile created alluring dimples in her cheeks. "There's no way I can make such a trip."

''Why not?'' He thought he'd just convinced her she could.

''I'll die of hypothermia. I didn't bring the kind of clothes needed for that kind of exposure.''

''No problem.''

''Freezing might not be a problem for you, but it doesn't appeal to me at all.''

''Wait here,'' Ross told her.

Fiona kept a wardrobe of special gear for guests who arrived unprepared for the rigors of the Montana winter. Ross had only to gather the proper garments Jessica would need for the snowmobile trip and hope they fit.

Experiencing a surge of self-satisfaction, he strode toward the storage closet at the end of the upstairs hall. He'd accomplished his major objective in persuading Jessica to stay until Wednesday.

Now all he had to do was keep her safe.

Chapter Eight

Jessica climbed the steps to the porch of the summer camp house and flexed her muscles, stiff from the long ride. The camp house sat on the crest of a ridge and a breathtaking winter wonderland stretched below her, as far as she could see.

The snowmobile ride had been long and noisy, vibrating every part of her until she wondered if she'd ever stop quivering. The heavy protective garments had barely kept out the cold, and she felt frozen to her bones. And despite the incredible stillness of the snow-covered scene, her ears still rang from the roar of the engines.

Cold, shaken and stiff, she should be miserable. But she wasn't, she realized with amazement. She was having the time of her life.

Not that sitting pressed against Ross with her arms wrapped around his waist and her face buried in his back had had anything to do with her exhilaration. It had to be the fantastic scenery, the wide open spaces, the brilliant sunshine and the crisp air, redolent with the scent of pines.

You hate winter, she reminded herself.

But, surprisingly, she was discovering it wasn't so bad, at least not in small doses.

Or as long as you have a man like Ross McGarrett to share it with.

She thrust that seductive thought aside, stomped the snow from her boots, stripped off her goggles and turned from the sweeping view to the house.

"This place looks like the Ponderosa," she said, remembering reruns of the old *Bonanza* series. The long, low rustic log building with its wide porch was what she had expected upon her arrival at the Shooting Star instead of the stately Victorian.

"Wait'll you see inside." Ross unlocked the door and held it open for her. "It'll take time to warm the place. I'll get the fires started."

Jessica entered the dim room. Ross followed, closed the door and began removing dustcovers from the furniture. Massive stone fireplaces flanked either end of the huge space. Its floor was made up of wide pine planks the color of pumpkin, and its principal furniture a long trestle table with benches and several leather sofas and chairs grouped in front of the fireplaces. A kitchen area with a wood-burning stove, a sink with an old-fashioned pump, and rustic pine counters and cabinets were tucked in one corner.

"No electricity or running water," Ross explained, "but we manage without them."

He quickly put matches to kindling and logs already laid in the twin fireplaces, then started a fire in the woodstove.

"Your crew lives here during the summer?" Jessica asked.

Ross nodded. "Sleeping quarters are upstairs in the loft—but the hands usually sleep outside near the herd if the weather's mild."

"And the place just sits empty the rest of the year?"

He raised an eyebrow. "You find that fiscally irresponsible?"

Surprised that her assignment had fled her mind completely, she said, "I left my financial hat back at the ranch. I'm merely curious."

"It's used sometimes for hunting parties or as a family retreat." Ross scanned the room with a glint in his eyes that told Jessica the place was special to him. "Fiona likes to come here to spend a few days alone, reading and enjoying the solitude. She says it recharges her batteries." He frowned, and his brown eyes darkened to almost black. "But I've discouraged her from staying here by herself since Kathy died last year."

In the excitement of the snowmobile ride, Jessica had forgotten the killer who stalked them. She was suddenly aware of how far she was from everyone and everything, and she felt isolated and vulnerable. She'd been a fool to let Ross talk her out of leaving Montana today.

She'd been an even bigger fool to allow him to carry her off into the wilderness.

What on earth had she been thinking?

Thinking?

Rational thought had nothing to do with her decision. After his simple kiss had created such a tumult of emotions in her last night, she'd been operating on some euphoric plane that was completely alien and impulsive. The last place she should be in her present state was alone.

With him.

As if sensing her thoughts, he came to her. Placing one arm around her shoulders, he tipped her face upward with his other hand until their eyes met. His gaze was warm, comforting, and she found herself drowning in deep brown eyes.

"You're safe here," he said softly. "I promise."

His words generated conflicting responses. On the one hand, she felt assured that he'd protect her with his life from anyone or anything that attempted to harm her. On the other, Ross McGarrett himself presented the greatest danger to the barriers she'd erected around her heart. She'd learned that lesson last night, when she'd longed to throw herself into his arms and have him sweep her off her feet. And the danger had reasserted itself this morning when her heart had leaped with happiness at the sight of him at her door.

That was exactly the kind of illogical, irrational,

junk-for-brains thinking that could lead to disastrous consequences.

Fighting against her absurd desire to remain in his embrace, she slipped from beneath his arm, moved toward one of the fireplaces and pointed to the antlers mounted above the mantel.

''Are those from deer?'' she said, grasping at the first subject that entered her mind to push memories of last night's kiss away.

''Elk,'' Ross said.

''You kill them for their antlers?'' she asked with a shudder.

He shook his head. ''Some folks hunt elk for food, but the venison's too gamy for my taste. Those antlers, however, came from a live elk. They shed them every year.'' He flashed her a grin. ''No animals were harmed or killed in the furnishing of this ranch house.''

''Oh, yeah?'' she challenged. ''How about the leather on these sofas?''

''Must be vinyl,'' he said with a deadpan expression.

''On a cattle ranch? Yeah, right.''

At least the atmosphere had lightened, and she'd managed to place some distance between them. Maybe she'd survive this outing after all without making a fool of herself again.

The fires were spreading warmth through the room, and Jessica found herself sweating in the heavy outerwear that had protected her from the windchill during her ride. She removed the head gear, jacket and pants and folded them across a nearby chair.

Ross did the same. "How about lunch?" he asked.

She cast a dubious glance at the primitive kitchen. "You're going to cook?"

He laughed, and she was struck again by how much she liked the rich, smooth sound of his voice.

"I've cooked many a meal here," he said, "but today you're in luck. I have a thermal hamper in the snowmobile. Chang Soo packed lunch for us."

He went outside and returned immediately with a hamper he must have stored beneath the seat of the vehicle. It had been several hours since breakfast, and the fresh air and frigid temperatures had made Jessica hungry.

"Want some help?" she offered.

"You're the guest today," he said. "Have a seat close to the fire, and I'll serve you."

He placed the hamper on a low table in front of the fireplace, then crossed to the corner kitchen. He carried back speckled-blue enameled plates, mugs and flatware, and, after covering a part of the table with a linen cloth Chang Soo had included in the hamper, set two places.

The hamper yielded a treasure trove of Chang Soo's specialties—sandwiches made of chunky chicken salad with almonds on thick slices of home-made bread, a hot compote of baked apples, apricots and raisins, and a large thermos bottle of fragrant, steaming coffee.

While they ate, Ross told her stories of past events at the summer camp, from bears raiding the garbage pit to the time a porcupine had cornered Fiona in the outhouse. He seemed the happiest and most relaxed he'd been since Jessica met him.

"You love the Shooting Star, don't you?" she asked, even though the answer was obvious.

"It's been my home my whole life," he said with a nod of agreement. "I can't imagine living anywhere else."

"But being sheriff takes so much of your time. Why not be just a full-time rancher?"

His expression sobered. "Some men see being sheriff as a stepping-stone to another elective office. They want to be a state senator, serve on the governor's cabinet, or even run for Congress."

"And you don't?" With his charm and good looks, Jessica figured he'd win any election in a landslide.

"I've never had political aspirations. I just want to keep life safe and orderly for the people I've known all my life."

She twisted in her chair to face him. "Don't take this wrong, but if that's your goal, what are you doing up here today with me? Shouldn't you be working?"

He nodded toward the radio on the sofa beside him. "I am working. Before we left this morning, I coordinated an investigation that reaches into eight states. Every detective in the Swenson County Department has an assignment. In order to identify the person who threatened you and find the others who've been terrorizing our citizens, we need information.''

''You can't catch your criminal if you don't know who he is,'' Jessica agreed.

''And I talked to Max.''

''How is he?''

''Max is fine. Nothing out of the ordinary with him or his family. He sent his love, by the way.''

''Did you tell him I was quitting?''

Ross appeared surprised. ''I didn't know you were.''

''You did, too,'' she said, less irritated than she'd expected, ''but it's just as well. I should tell him myself so he can line up a replacement.''

''Maybe you'll change your mind.'' Ross leaned over and refilled her coffee cup.

''And maybe pigs will fly.''

He shrugged. ''Stranger things have happened.''

''I expect to board a plane to Miami on Wednesday,'' she stated firmly, wondering if she was trying to convince herself as much as Ross. She was growing to like the sheriff too much for her own good, and placing three thousand miles between them seemed a smart idea.

''Kathy didn't particularly like the Shooting Star,

either," Ross said. "She fell in love with New York. Wanted to live in the city."

"It's not that I don't *like* your ranch," Jessica said hastily.

"It's a nice place to visit, but you wouldn't want to live here?"

"My Florida blood's too thin. I'd never survive an entire winter."

She expected him to argue, but instead, he stood and placed more logs on the fire.

"You must miss Kathy a great deal," Jessica said.

Talking about his wife should help reerect those barriers around her emotions, she hoped. The man was a widower with a child, still grieving over the tragic death of his pretty, young wife. He didn't have the time or inclination for involvement with a stranger.

Not that she was interested.

"There's a lot you don't know," Ross answered.

"And it's none of my business," Jessica assured him quickly. "After all, I'm just a hired hand, not really your guest."

"I'd like you to be a friend." Ross sank back onto the sofa and pierced her with a searching gaze. "For the past year, it's been hard to know who my real friends are, since there's a high probability one of them killed Kathy."

"If I'm to do my job," Jessica said quickly, "I have to remain objective—"

"Didn't you just tell me you're quitting and going home?"

"Yes, but—"

"Then be my friend until you leave."

"But I hardly know you."

"That's why I brought you here. So we can get to know each other better."

The heat in his eyes made the room suddenly too warm, and she fought the urge to rise and move away from the fire. She tore her gaze from his, afraid of what she saw there. "I don't have time for many friends in my line of work. I move around a lot."

"And that suits you?"

Jessica started to answer in the affirmative, then stopped. Did she really like bouncing from one location to another, staying in unfamiliar cities, sleeping in hotels, dining alone in restaurants? She had her condo, but spent little time there. She realized with a start that she stayed so busy, she'd never taken time to analyze whether she was doing what she wanted with her life.

But what was the alternative? A husband? Children? And the all-too-familiar heartbreak when that arrangement eventually came crashing down around her?

"Tell me about Kathy." She was unwilling to talk about herself, reluctant to examine her own life too closely.

Ross leaned his head against the back of the sofa and closed his eyes. For a moment, Jessica thought he wouldn't answer. When he opened his eyes, their brown depths reflected pain and sadness.

"Kathy," he said softly, "was a terrible mistake."

His words jolted Jessica. Then she recalled Fiona's reference to Kathy as a disaster and realized that she shouldn't have asked. She felt like an interloper into the McGarrett family secrets. "Maybe you shouldn't be telling me this."

"I need to talk to someone," he said. "The only other person who knows the whole truth is Fiona."

Jessica took a deep breath and resigned herself to hearing his story. If Ross needed to get something off his chest, maybe she was the logical choice, like travelers who share secrets on a journey, then part, never to meet again.

"I'm listening," she said.

He sat up, leaned forward and clasped his hands between his knees. His gaze never left the fireplace, and the dancing flames were reflected in his eyes.

"Courtney isn't my daughter."

"What?"

Nothing he said could have surprised her more. Jessica had never witnessed more fatherly love and devotion than Ross had shown for the little girl.

"I'm her legal father," he explained. "My name is on her birth certificate. And I couldn't love her more if she were my own blood, but I'm not her biological father."

"I see." But Jessica didn't see at all. She'd have to wait for Ross to explain.

"As long as I can remember," Ross said, still staring at the fire, "I wanted my own family, a wife and children to fill all the big, empty rooms at the Shooting Star with laughter and love."

"And that's where Kathy came in?"

"Not at first. I spent years looking for the right woman."

"Your soul mate?" Jessica couldn't keep the irony from her voice. She'd lost track of her father's and mother's "soul mates," none of whom had lasted very long.

If he heard her sarcasm, he ignored it. "Crazy as it sounds, yes. I always felt there's a woman out there who was meant to spend the rest of her life with me."

"And then you found Kathy?"

He shook his head. "Remember Jack Randall? You met him at the Chandlers' last night."

"The tall, lanky man who wants to contest your northern boundaries?"

"He's Kathy's father."

"Your father-in-law?"

"I remember when Kathy was born. Watched her grow up on the neighboring ranch, a skinny, irritating kid who was crazy about dogs and horses. She was always hanging around. Any excuse to get away from home."

"And when she grew up, you fell in love with her?"

"There was never any love between Kathy and me."

"Oh." Jessica didn't know what else to say.

Ross leaned back, stretched his long legs toward the fire and crossed his boots at his ankles. "Jack and Margaret Randall are about as straitlaced and uptight as any people I've ever met. Pious to the extreme. Everything is black and white with them. Kathy was their only child and they kept her on a short leash. Rarely allowed her out of their sight. Had a list of dos and don'ts a mile long the poor kid had to follow or there was hell to pay."

"Doesn't sound like a Norman Rockwell childhood." Jessica had never stopped to think that having parents around all the time might be worse than not having them there at all.

Ross grimaced. "Kathy was bound to rebel."

"By marrying you?"

His expression saddened. "She had barely turned eighteen when she came to see me. She was in a horrible mess and needed my help."

Jessica considered the strong, competent man before her. If she was ever in a mess, she'd want a man like Ross McGarrett to go to.

"She was three months pregnant," Ross said. "The father was an itinerant cowhand who'd worked at their ranch, then disappeared two months earlier. Kathy wanted me to find him so he could marry her. Otherwise, she said, her father would kill her for dishonoring him."

"You couldn't locate the cowhand?"

"I found him all right," Ross said grimly.

"But he wouldn't marry her?"

"Couldn't. He was dead. Killed in a logging accident in Kalispell four days before I tracked him down."

"How awful."

"Maybe not as awful for Kathy as if he'd married her. The man had rap sheets in three states. He would have made a terrible husband—and an even worse father."

"So you married Kathy out of pity?" Jessica found that concept hard to accept.

"More like selfishness. I'd given up on finding the woman of my dreams. I wasn't getting any younger, and I've always wanted children at the ranch. Kathy was a sweet kid. If marrying her provided me with an instant family and got her out of a jam… Well, it seemed a good idea at the time."

"But I'm guessing it didn't make Jack Randall happy," Jessica said, remembering the man's angry attitude toward Ross at the party.

"Jack, being Jack, immediately assumed the worst. That I'd gotten his young daughter pregnant as part of some master plot to take over his ranch."

"She didn't tell him about the real father?" Jessica asked in disbelief.

"We decided not to. We didn't want any stigma attached to the baby."

Jessica had already recognized that Ross was

brave and competent. Now she added noble and unselfish to his list of attributes. "Is your feud with Jack why you called Kathy a terrible mistake?"

"Jack's the kind of man who'll always find a reason to fight with his neighbors," Ross said. "No, the mistake was both of us marrying without love."

"But you knew that going into the marriage."

Ross nodded. "In some cultures, all marriages are arranged and love isn't an issue. But often love grows out of those arrangements. It didn't in our case."

"But you had Courtney."

His expression softened, and Jessica wished for one fleeting moment that someone somewhere someday would look like that at the mention of her name.

"Courtney made it all worthwhile," Ross said. "For me, at least."

"But not for Kathy?"

"Kathy was too young, too emotionally scarred as a result of her parents' abuse to bond with Courtney. The child only made her nervous. All Kathy wanted was to escape. From Montana. From Courtney. From me."

He sighed, sat upright and pushed his fingers through his hair. "She escaped all right."

Jessica caught her breath. "You don't think she tampered with her own brakes?"

"Suicide?" Ross shook his head. "She was looking·forward to a different life too much to take her own. If she'd lived, we could have worked something out. An amicable separation. Even a divorce, if she'd wanted. Now…'' His voice trailed off sadly.

''Have you investigated Jack Randall?'' Jessica asked.

''For his daughter's death?''

''You said Kathy was afraid he'd kill her for dishonoring him with her out-of-wedlock pregnancy.''

''I've considered that possibility,'' he admitted grudgingly.

''And?''

''Jack's a pain in the ass, but he wouldn't murder his own daughter.''

Jessica recalled the anger seething in the rancher she'd met at the Chandlers'. ''But a man like that wouldn't think twice about coming after the person he sees as the source of all his problems, would he?''

''Everyone's a suspect until we find our would-be killer,'' Ross said, ''but as much as Jack irritates me, I'd hate to think it's him. He's Courtney's grandfather, after all.''

''So you still believe someone killed Kathy to get at you?'' Jessica asked.

''It fits the pattern. The home invasion at the judge's house, a burglary at the mayor's office, the intimidation of the county clerk. All are government officials.''

''But has an official or a member of their family been the object of every crime?''

''No.'' Ross's voice heavy with frustration. ''Nothing's that clear-cut.''

"So you could be looking for freedom fighters—"

"SCOFF," Ross said with a scowl.

"Or several different criminals?"

Ross tossed her a wry smile. "If we knew who we were looking for, we'd just go get them."

"It must be a frustrating job," Jessica said with sympathy. "At least in my work, all the facts I need are there. I just have to wade through them, not go find them. Are you certain you don't want to stick with ranching alone?"

"Alone?" He raised her head and stared at her with a look she couldn't fathom. "Not alone. I'm still searching for a woman to share my life, to help me fill the Shooting Star with children."

Jessica resisted the urge to squirm under the intensity of his gaze. "I'm sure you'll find her someday."

"I believe I already have."

The impact of his words jolted her to her feet. "I hope you're not talking about me."

She started to move away, but he grasped her hand and held her fast. "Something clicked the day I met you."

"Yeah—" She tried to pull away again. "That maniac Santa's shotgun."

"It was more than that," he insisted in a low, firm voice that didn't *sound* crazy. "You're unlike any woman I've ever known."

"But you don't know me." Her voice rose an octave in desperation. She wasn't sure what was happening. Her heart was beating like a rock band's drummer on speed, and the rush of blood to her head was making her dizzy. "You can't know me. We only met three days ago."

The tenderness in his expression threatened to melt her defenses. "I feel as if I've known you all my life."

With a gentle tug that she was too weakened by surprise to resist, he pulled her onto his lap. His face was inches from hers. His scent filled her nostrils, an exhilarating mix of leather, sunshine and masculinity. Before she could react, Ross slid his arms around her and drew her against the hard muscles of his chest. She could feel his heartbeat, even through several layers of clothing. His lips claimed hers, and with dismay, she found herself opening her mouth to his.

Trembling with delight, as if every nerve ending in her body was connected to that kiss, she arched against him, absorbing his heat. He threaded his fingers through her hair to hold her close. Long before she was ready, he pulled away and cupped her face in his hands. His brown eyes, smoky with desire, peered into hers.

"Tell me you didn't feel anything," he challenged her.

"I...I'm not sure," she hedged, unwilling to admit even to herself how much his kiss had shaken her.

The lips that had sent her senses into chaos seconds before lifted in a broad grin. "Then we'd better try it again, until you're certain."

Too befuddled by the emotions that flooded her, Jessica didn't protest when he lowered his mouth to hers. And she couldn't hold back the soft moan of pleasure that escaped her when he slid his hands beneath her sweater and caressed the bare skin of her back. She wrapped her arms around his neck, molding her body to his.

He tugged her sideways until they lay side by side on the sofa, their legs entwined. Desire exploded inside her, a seething cauldron of need.

Again, Ross pulled away, propping himself on his elbows to look down at her. "Feel anything yet?"

His eyes held a twinkle, but his voice was breathless, as if he'd been running long and hard.

Jessica couldn't deny the effect he'd had on her, but she refused to succumb to her emotions. She'd spent too much of her life protecting herself from feelings that could lead to love. And loss.

"It's just sex," she insisted, avoiding his eyes. "Touch the right buttons, and you'll get the same result from anyone."

"Okay," he said, entirely too agreeably, "we'll take sex out of the equation. How about I just hold you and we talk?"

Disappointment cascaded through her. Her body ached for him. No, not for Ross, she assured herself. Just for the release of sexual tension. Sexual excitement wasn't the same as love.

When he pulled her against him like nesting spoons, gently smoothed her hair from her face and held her lightly in his arms, she couldn't deny the overwhelming feeling of coming home, of being where she'd always wanted to be, in a place she'd been searching for all her life.

"Comfy?" he asked.

"Mmm." She nestled against him, ignoring the alarm bells ringing in her head, warning that she was going too far too fast, and that she'd soon reach the point of no return.

"You should see the Shooting Star in the spring and summer," Ross said. "Acres of wildflowers blooming on the prairies, miles of green grass, fresh air, warm breezes—"

"What are you?" she asked in a teasing tone. "Head of local tourism?"

"I'd like to show you the ranch in all its seasons. I know you don't like winter, but it's not always cold here."

She wasn't cold now. She was warm and relaxed in his arms, feeling as if she could stay there forever.

Had she lost her mind?

No emotional involvement, remember?

But these emotions felt so good, so right, how could she resist?

Luckily, fate stepped in to save her.

The radio on the sofa crackled to life with the no-nonsense female dispatcher's voice Jessica recognized from the day of her accident. "Sheriff, we have a problem."

Ross released her and sat up. Jessica stood and

moved away as he grabbed the radio and depressed the key. "What's up, Shirley?"

"That rifle you sent Deputy Greenlea to collect from Judge Chandler?"

"Is it a ballistics match?"

"We may never know. It's been stolen."

Chapter Nine

"Damn!" Ross muttered to himself, then spoke into the radio mike. "Get a Crime Scene Unit to the judge's house."

"They're on their way, sir," Shirley responded. "Deputy Greenlea already called them."

"I'll be there as soon as possible," Ross said.

He glanced across the room where Jessica was already tugging on her gear. The dispatch call couldn't have come at a worse time. Ross had finally felt he was making headway, breaking through the barriers Jessica kept around herself. He'd even hoped to talk her into staying through Christmas.

And maybe forever.

The theft of Harry's rifle blew that discussion to hell. It also pointed the finger directly at Dixon Traxler. Why else would someone steal the rifle the man had been using, if not to cover an attempted murder?

Remembering Jessica in his arms, the warmth of her body, the sweetness of her breath, the silkiness of her skin, Ross reached for his own gear with regret. At least he could console himself with the fact that he'd kept her safe.

So far.

If Traxler was after her, he could have followed her to Miami. The ex-con would have a hard time doing that when Ross threw him in jail. But the sheriff would need probable cause for any charges to stick. That's why he hoped Traxler had screwed up at the Chandlers' and left evidence of his theft. Not every criminal was as wily as the ones Ross had been tracking the past year.

He grabbed the radio. "Shirley, ask the judge for a warrant to search Traxler's hotel room and vehicle. The sooner the better."

"Ten-four, boss."

Jessica looked at him wide-eyed. "You believe Traxler stole the rifle?"

"Seems too much a coincidence otherwise." Ross grabbed the hamper. "You ready?"

She nodded and followed him outside. On the porch, she hesitated. "You think he might be tracking us, planning to shoot?"

Ross shook his head. "I doubt he'd use the rifle again. The whole point of stealing it is to break the connection to him."

"You're sure Traxler stole it?"

He shrugged. "Can't be sure of anything until I have evidence to back me up. But my gut tells me that missing rifle is somehow connected to the attempt on your life."

She tilted her head and gazed up at him with a look that made him want to sweep her into his arms, carry her back inside and make love to her until his eyes crossed.

She was obviously unaware of the effect she had on him. "What if someone wanted to cast suspicion on Traxler," she asked, "by stealing the gun he's been using?"

Ross gazed at her with respect. "You'd make a good law officer."

"I'm just an armchair detective," she admitted. "I don't have the stomach for the real thing."

"I'd put you up against my best deputies," he said without hesitation. "You've more than proven you have the guts for the job."

"Then why are my knees shaking at the thought of riding back to the Shooting Star on an open snowmobile?"

He grinned, leaned over and kissed her lightly on the lips. "I said you were brave. I never said you were stupid."

She touched her gloves to her lips and considered him with narrowed eyes. "I'm beginning to wonder."

"Stupid would be standing out here in the cold continuing this discussion," he said. "Let's get back to the ranch."

THREE HOURS LATER, Ross and Jessica were climbing the steps to the Chandlers' front door. The Crime

Scene van was parked out front, and every light in the house was ablaze.

Julie opened the door for them. "Come join the party," she said with a rueful smile, "such as it is."

Ross gave her a quick hug before shedding his coat. "You've been through enough already, Julie. I'm sorry you're having to endure this, too."

"Glad to see you again, Jessica," Julie said. "Come in by the fire. Harry's made mulled wine, and I've put together some sandwiches."

"Thanks." Jessica tugged off her coat, looking stunningly beautiful in spite of the ordeal she was experiencing.

Ross knew too well how it felt to be hunted by an unknown foe. He hoped tonight to put an end to her fears by locking Traxler up again, this time for life.

"Ross, Jessica." Harry greeted them in the living room and handed them mugs of spicy hot wine. "You're just in time. Josh and Don have finished their investigations."

Josh Greenlea and Don Parker, the crime tech, were already seated near the fire where Julie served them sandwiches from a heaping platter.

Jessica perched on an arm of the sofa, and Ross stood with his back to the fire, confronting his men.

"What have you got?" he asked.

Don, his mouth full of ham and cheese, nodded for Josh to go first.

"Traxler's clean," the deputy said.

Ross felt his mouth drop in surprise. "You're sure?"

Josh nodded. "We didn't get a warrant—"

Ross whipped around to Harry. "Why not?"

The judge, relaxing in his favorite chair, smiled indulgently. "Didn't need one. I asked Dixon to cooperate. He did."

Ross looked back to Josh. "You did a thorough search?"

Greenlea nodded. "Car and hotel room. No sign of the judge's rifle."

Parker swallowed and wiped his mouth with a napkin. "Nothing here at the house that's helpful, either. The gun cabinet was wiped clean. Not a print anywhere."

"Hairs? Fibers?" Ross demanded.

"So many it'll take weeks to process them," Parker said. "There was a party here last night. Must have been a hundred different people in and out of the house before the festivities ended."

"So the gun could have been taken then?" Ross asked the judge.

"It's possible," Harry said. "I didn't check the cabinet until Josh came by for the gun this afternoon."

"And the one rifle is all that's missing?" Jessica asked, the strain evident on her face.

The judge nodded.

"And that was the only .223-caliber rifle in the house," Greenlea said. "The same one he'd loaned

Traxler. The thief left other more expensive guns behind, so profit wasn't a motive.''

''Has Traxler been interrogated?'' Ross asked.

''The detectives are having a go at him now,'' Greenlea said. ''But I'm afraid they'll have to release him.''

''There's more bad news?'' Ross asked.

Greenlea looked glum. ''He has an alibi for Saturday morning when the shooting occurred.''

''Airtight?'' Ross demanded.

''Seems to be,'' Josh said with obvious regret. ''The owner of the hotel delivered room service to Traxler within minutes of the time the shot was fired at the ranch.''

Ross nodded. Greg Stickland, the hotel's owner, was a straight shooter, as unlikely a candidate to have been coerced or bought off by Traxler as anyone Ross knew. ''The alibi only means Traxler didn't fire the shot himself. It doesn't mean he didn't hire someone else to do it.''

''See here, Ross,'' Harry interjected. ''I keep telling you Dixon's a changed man. He regrets his previous crimes and he isn't about to commit others.''

Ross turned to Julie. ''That your opinion, too?''

Julie cast her husband an apologetic glance. ''I don't know Dixon as well as Harry does. Their friendship began before I ever met my husband.''

Josh pushed to his feet. ''Anything else you need from me tonight, Sheriff?''

Parker stood also. ''I'm through here, too.''

"Thanks for your help," Ross said. "I'll see you both in my office tomorrow."

The deputy and technician left, and the judge waved Ross toward a chair. "Take a load off, Ross. It's been a rough few days."

"It's been a rough year." Ross sat down, but he declined the sandwich Julie offered. His appetite was gone, killed by frustration. He gazed across the room at his friend. "I don't know what's happening in this county, Harry, but I sure as hell intend to find out."

"Looks like you've reached a dead end," Jessica said with clear sympathy.

Ross turned to her, and the sight warmed his heart. He'd continue his investigation, no matter how many roadblocks he hit. Someone had killed his wife, terrorized his friends and neighbors, and was now threatening a woman who'd finagled her way into his heart. He wasn't about to quit searching for the culprits.

"We're still investigating," he said. "Something will turn up. Whoever's responsible for all this isn't perfect. He—"

"Or she," Julie added.

"—will make a mistake," Ross said. "And that mistake will lead us to him. Or her."

The judge raised his mug in a grim toast. "Let's just pray no one else is harmed in the meantime."

TWO DAYS LATER, Jessica sat in Ross's office and contemplated the surrounding space with satisfaction.

Gone were the stacks of file folders and papers that had covered the floor and were strewn across every flat surface the first night she had seen the room. While Ross had been busy with his investigation, she'd organized the chaos in his office. She'd been thankful for the grueling job because it had kept her too busy to think.

About Ross.

Or whoever was trying to kill her.

Not that she hadn't felt safe. With several ranch hands patrolling outside the house and a special deputy assigned to a security detail inside, she'd had nothing to fear. A would-be assassin would need a strong death wish to attempt any harm at the ranch under such conditions.

With the exceptional security, Jessica had no valid reason not to stay and complete her assignment for Max.

Except Ross.

Maybe what she felt for him was just sexual attraction, but whatever it was, the pull was too dangerous, too strong. If she wasn't careful, she'd find herself opening not only her body but her heart and soul to him, too. She hadn't avoided emotional entanglements most of her life only to capitulate to the first handsome cowboy she'd ever met. She didn't want to fall in love only to have her heart broken. She'd watched that scenario play out with her parents too many times.

Sure, she'd miss the heights of passion, but she'd

also miss the pits of despair. Her simple, uncomplicated life suited her fine. She wasn't about to let the
charismatic lawman—or anybody else—change that.

"Hi, Jess'ca."

Breaking free of her contemplation, Jessica
glanced up from the clutter-free desktop to find
Courtney in the doorway, a small book clasped tight
in her chubby hands. For the past three nights, the
little girl had insisted that Jessica, and no one else,
read her a story before bedtime. Jessica was surprised
to find herself looking forward to the ritual, the
warmth of Courtney's tiny body scrunched against
her side, the sloppy good-night kisses the child
pressed on her, the unconditional affection so clearly
demonstrated by the little girl's smiles and hugs.

Amazingly, Courtney seemed to fill that deep, bar-
ren emotional hole Jessica had experienced all her
life, the wasteland where her parents' love should
have been, and she couldn't deny the burgeoning affection she felt for Ross's tiny daughter.

"Have you picked a book?" Jessica asked.

"Uh-huh." Courtney scurried into the room,
climbed onto the sofa and tucked her nightgown
around her feet.

Jessica pushed away from the desk and joined the
girl, experiencing a jolt of tenderness when Courtney
handed her the book and cuddled against her side.
The child was so affectionate, so trusting, so vulnerable that Jessica's heart ached for her. To be so
young without a mother—

Jessica swallowed the lump in her throat and opened the book. "*Pat the Bunny*. Is this a new book?"

Courtney shook her head, her golden curls whipping her face. "It's old."

"Well, it's new to me." All children's literature was new to her, Jessica realized with a start. She couldn't remember her parents ever reading to her, and she'd never had a child to read to before. "Let's start."

"You gots a bunny?" Courtney asked.

Jessica shook her head.

"A kitty-cat?"

"No," Jessica answered. "And no doggie, either."

Courtney's expression was mournful. "And no toys?"

"I'm a big girl. I don't need toys."

But Courtney's question jarred loose a memory of a stuffed toy, a well-worn Scottie with a frayed tartan bow, that Jessica had carried to boarding school that first year and hidden under her pillow so the other girls wouldn't tease her about it. She'd named the dog Mac, and his soft plush covering had absorbed many of Jessica's late-night tears.

"I gots a teddy bear," Courtney said, "named Sammy."

"I'd like to meet Sammy sometime," Jessica said, wondering if Courtney held her teddy at night while crying for her dead mother. Giving the girl an extra hug, she began to read.

A while later, after Jessica's reading through the book and Courtney's patting the bunny and following the other assorted directions many times, the girl stood on the sofa beside Jessica and twined her arms around her neck.

"Wuv you, Jess'ca," the child whispered in her ear.

At the sound of those words, something warm and wonderful clutched at Jessica's heart. "I love you, too, Courtney."

"Cupcake," Ross corrected. He stood on the threshold, his tall body filling the doorway, and observed them with a strange expression.

Courtney looked to her father and giggled. "Cour'ney, not Cupcake."

"Whatever your name is—" Fiona entered, slipping into the room behind Ross "—it's bedtime. Come, I'll tuck you in."

"Want Jess'ca." Courtney tightened her hold on Jessica's neck.

Before Jessica could offer to fulfill the child's request, Ross said, "I need to talk with Jessica. Let Granny tuck you in tonight."

Courtney's lower lip protruded, a prelude to a pout.

"I'll tuck you in tomorrow night," Jessica promised. "Okay?"

"'Kay." Courtney kissed her cheek, hugged her tighter with an audible grunt, then released her and scampered down to join her great-grandmother.

When the two had left, Ross turned to her. "Does that mean you're staying?"

"What?"

"Tomorrow's Wednesday. How can you tuck in Courtney if you're on a plane to Miami?"

"Oh, my gosh. I forgot."

"Memory lapse?"

"Brain fatigue."

"Maybe you want to stay and won't admit it." The look he threw her was challenging.

He had her pegged, all right. More than anything, she wanted to stay. With him and with Courtney. Which was exactly the reason why she wouldn't.

She opened her mouth to reiterate that she would leave as planned. "I—"

"Don't say anything yet."

Ross crossed the room in three long strides and sat beside her on the sofa. They didn't touch, but she could feel his body heat and resisted the urge to scoot closer.

"I have a favor to ask first," Ross said.

She raised an eyebrow and considered him. Ross wasn't the kind of man who liked to place himself in anyone's debt.

As if reading her thoughts, he said with a pleading expression, "I'm not used to asking favors, but this is important."

"I can't make any promises if I don't know what the favor is."

"Are you comfortable here?" he asked.

"Who wouldn't be? The house is lovely, and Fiona is a perfect hostess."

He shook his head, his lips curving in a slight smile that was entirely too appealing. "By comfortable, I meant secure, protected. Have you felt concern for your safety the last few days?"

"None whatsoever," Jessica answered honestly. "Fort Knox couldn't be better guarded than the Shooting Star."

"Good," Ross said with a nod of satisfaction. "That makes my request easier."

Having a good guess at what he was about to say, Jessica waited, intending to say no.

"As you've probably noticed," Ross continued, "I've been busy lately."

Jessica nodded again. The man had been skillfully coordinating a huge investigation involving law enforcement agencies from Florida to Montana and Chicago to New York and California.

"If you return to Miami and Max has to send someone else in your place," Ross said, "I won't have time to bring a newcomer up to speed on the ranch."

"Can't Fiona do that?"

"Until I find the people responsible for Kathy's death, your car accident, and Saturday's shooting, I'd rather Fiona stick close to home—and stay inside as much as possible."

"So you're asking me to remain long enough to complete the evaluation of the ranch's financial status?" She felt her face flush. By having her admit up front that she felt secure, he'd already undercut her major excuse for leaving.

"That will give me more time to devote to my duties and help keep Fiona safe," he said somberly.

She felt suddenly trapped, and like a cornered animal, her temper flared. "You really know how to lay on a guilt trip."

"No one's forcing you to stay," he said, so reasonably it made her even angrier. "I've already said I'll take you to Billings for your flight tomorrow, if that's what you want. And you don't owe me anything, so you're under no coercion to grant my request."

Jessica squirmed. Not owe him anything? She owed him her life, which he'd saved twice in one day. How small-minded and mean-spirited would she appear if she said no?

And do you care? an inner voice argued. *What's Ross to you that his opinion matters?*

Nothing, she wanted to respond, but she couldn't bring herself to believe that. She respected the man, as much as she respected Max, who was at the top of her list. She'd seen Ross's selflessness in the bank when he dived in front of a shotgun blast to protect her. What would a couple more weeks in Montana matter? Especially if she stayed indoors, warm and safe.

If Ross remained as busy as he'd been the last two days, his presence shouldn't be a problem. She could bury herself in reports and accounts and forget he existed. And she wouldn't have to face Max and make flimsy excuses for running away from a man who stirred her senses too much for comfort.

"Well?" Ross asked gently.

"I'm still thinking," she hedged.

With a tender smile that made her ache with sudden longing, he delivered the coup de grâce. "In addition to freeing up my time, your being here is really good for Courtney, especially since I have to be away so much."

She really had lost her mind. Maybe it was because the air was thinner in Montana's altitude, and her brain wasn't getting enough oxygen. Ms. Can't-stand-rug-rats had turned to jelly at the mere thought of Courtney's unhappiness.

The little girl would survive, she assured herself, trying to harden her heart. Sure, the kid would be lonely for a while, but she'd get over it once Ross's case was solved, his workload eased, and her daddy was able to spend more time with her.

"Still thinking?" Ross prodded.

She felt another surge of anger, this time at herself. She was walking, eyes wide open, into exactly the kind of emotional quagmire she'd made a point of avoiding all her life. What had happened to her resolve?

Apparently her determination to stay uninvolved had been the first casualty when she'd been ambushed by a real live Western hero and his two-foot sidekick, a doll-baby named Cupcake.

Don't be a coward, her conscience scolded her. *Prove to yourself you can stay. Either tough it out and remain aloof or enjoy a brief fling and leave at the end of your job with no regrets.*

"You're sure you won't be around much?" she asked.

His face fell. "Is that a condition for your staying?"

"I'd need to concentrate on my work," she said quickly. "I couldn't be interrupted."

"What about Courtney?" Concern for his daughter softened the strong angles of his face. "She's awfully good at interrupting."

She reached deep inside, searching for her lost resolve. "Maybe I should just catch that plane tomorrow."

"Would it help to know that Traxler's leaving town tomorrow, too?"

"We've said all along Traxler could have hired out his dirty work," Jessica said. "So whether he's here or not is immaterial. Where's he going?"

"A twelve-city book tour."

Jessica grimaced. "Autographing copies of *A New Man, A New Life*?"

Ross nodded. "He starts in San Francisco and ends up in New York."

"Good. That'll keep him away from me."

"One of the twelve cities is Miami," Ross added. "A week from today."

Jessica cocked her head and confronted Ross. "You think he's still a danger to me?"

"Someone's a danger to you. You weren't run off the road and shot at on a whim. That's why I intend to keep you under guard as long as you're in my county."

He reached over and took her hand, twining his long, slender fingers with hers. "I meant what I said at the summer camp."

She fought against the urge to keep holding his hand. And lost. "You said a lot of things."

"You're a remarkable person, Jessica." His voice was low, seductive, and she wished he'd keep on talking so she could listen forever. "I want to know you better. I'm sorry things are in such turmoil that it's not possible right now."

"I have my work, too," she assured him. "And after that, I'll return to Miami. So there's no point in us getting to know each other better."

His gaze searched her face, and the flickering flames from the fireplace danced like golden flecks in his eyes.

"None at all?" he asked softly, leaning toward her.

She shook her head adamantly. "None…what… so…ev…"

He dipped his head, his lips closed over hers, and she suppressed a groan of pleasure. The heat from the fire had transferred to the core of her being. As if of their own volition, her arms circled his neck, and her mouth opened to his.

She was drowning in a sea of sensations. His distinctive masculine scent. The taste of coffee and fine whiskey on his tongue. The sound of his breathing, heavy and rapid. The touch of his hands skimming her body until every nerve ending tingled, hungry for more.

He pulled away and surveyed her face, as if memorizing what he saw. A smile tugged at the corners of his lips. "You're sure?"

The only thing she was sure of at the moment was that she was sorry he'd stopped kissing her. "About what?"

"No point in us knowing each other better."

"Absolutely."

"Well, I'm glad that's settled." Before she could register the irony in his voice, he was kissing her again.

And she was kissing him back.

With her reason overcome by pure pleasure, she couldn't think, didn't want to. All she wanted was more.

After several moments he drew back again. "You didn't give me an answer."

Disoriented, drunk with desire, she replied, "I did, too. I said, 'absolutely.'"

His face lit up like a Broadway marquee. "So you will stay and finish your assignment?"

She sat up, placed some distance between them and tried to make contact with her brain. It had obviously been hot-wired by too much sensory input. She opened her mouth to correct his misinterpretation, then closed it again.

She'd enjoyed kissing Ross, enjoyed it more than she'd ever enjoyed kissing anyone. And she was a big girl. If she wanted to stay, to spend some time in the luscious lawman's arms—although, as he'd said, his time was limited—where was the harm? When her job was finished, the three thousand miles between Miami and Montana would be an adequate impediment to further involvement.

"I can't let Max down," she heard herself saying, although Max was the furthest person from her thoughts at the moment.

Ross caressed her cheek. "Having you here means a great deal to me."

She purposely misread what his words, gesture and facial expression were telling her. "I'll give Courtney as much attention as I can."

Before matters progressed in a direction she wasn't ready for, she stood abruptly. "Tomorrow's a working day. For both of us. I'll say good night now."

He pushed to his feet, but she hurried from the room before he could touch her again. She didn't trust herself to risk another kiss, knowing where it would lead.

''Sleep well, Jessica,'' he called after her as she fled the office.

She hurried up the stairs to her room, afraid she'd weaken if she lingered. The cloying fragrance struck her the moment she opened the door, and even with the lights off, she knew someone had been in her room.

Thinking Fiona had changed the flower arrangements, Jessica flipped on the lights and closed the door behind her.

A crimson splotch on her pillow immediately caught her eye. A huge red satin bow and streamers decorated a spray of creamy-white gardenias nestled at the head of the bed. When she approached, she noticed the card attached with its typed note.

''Don't worry, Jessica. I'm watching you. Your secret Santa.''

Her thoughts flew immediately to Ross, and her heart warmed at the message. When she reached for the flowers, however, she pulled her hand back in alarm.

They were ice cold. Someone had either just removed them from refrigeration or brought them in from outside. Ross couldn't have done that. He'd spent the past half-hour with her in his office.

Her heart pounded to an entirely different beat from the one prompted by Ross's kisses. This rhythm pulsed with fear.

If Ross wasn't her secret Santa, who was?

And why was he watching her?

Chapter Ten

"You're up early." Ross greeted Jessica when she entered the dining room.

"Today's a working day," Jessica said as coolly as if they hadn't kissed the night before.

Maybe that contact hadn't impacted her as much as him, but he doubted it. He'd clearly felt her response last night, her sudden intake of breath, the quickening of her pulse, the heat of her skin—

"I like an early start," she added, dispersing his memories with her practical tone.

He didn't know why he felt so happy. A fast-moving cold front was flinging sleet against the windows. He had a list of unsolved crimes as long as his arm. Buck Bender had called the vet to come out for a look at his best breeding bull who was off his feed this morning. And Jessica had just greeted him with the politeness of a stranger.

In spite of all that, Ross was content, and the source of his happiness had just taken a seat across from him.

"Sleep okay?" he asked.

"Fine," Jessica replied too quickly, but she didn't appear rested.

He wondered what had kept her awake and caused the delicate shadows beneath her eyes, the slight nervous tremor of her hands. Second thoughts about staying in Montana? Regrets over kissing him?

She wasn't giving him any clues. She sipped the coffee that Chang Soo had just poured, then looked at Ross. "You know anything about gardenias?"

"They smell nice. Why?"

"Just wondering."

Ross studied Jessica, trying to decide the motive for her query. With other women, he'd have considered a comment about flowers an obvious hint, a hope Ross would respond with a gift bouquet. But Jessica didn't seem the type to make that kind of suggestion. She was too straightforward, not the type to play coy. Gardenias grew profusely in Miami's climate. Maybe her mention of them was merely a sign of homesickness.

"Mrs. McGarrett grows gardenias in the solarium," Chang Soo chimed in.

"She does?" Jessica said, clearly interested.

"But they not blooming now," Chang Soo added. "Maybe next month."

The chef returned to the kitchen, and Jessica turned to Ross with a puzzled expression. But before she could speak, his grandmother joined them.

Ross rose from his seat and pulled out his grandmother's chair while studying her with concern. "Are you feeling all right, Fiona? You're never up before ten o'clock. You're three hours early today."

His grandmother shook her linen napkin and spread it across her lap. "I have a great deal to do before we leave for the airport."

"Airport?" Ross asked in alarm and turned his attention to Jessica. "Last night you said you were staying."

Jessica looked confused. "I did. I am."

Fiona made a clucking noise with her tongue. "Jessica's not leaving, Ross. I am. And I'm taking Courtney with me."

"Whoa, doggies," Ross said. "What are you talking about?"

"Courtney and I are going to Walt Disney World," Fiona announced in a don't-argue-with-me tone.

"Orlando?" Jessica asked in surprise and threw Ross a searching glance.

He shrugged with an I-knew-nothing-about-this expression and returned his attention to his grandmother. "Ever think of consulting me before taking my daughter all the way across the country?"

The edge in his tone failed to rattle Fiona. "That's what I'm doing now. Consulting you."

"After you've already made the plans?" Ross said with more heat than he'd intended.

"My plans can be canceled if they don't suit you," Fiona said mildly and waited for Chang Soo to pour her coffee. "But I made them with you in mind."

After all these years, Fiona never ceased to surprise him. "I'm all ears," he said.

His grandmother leaned across the table and patted his hand, exactly as she'd done ever since he was a child. "I know how much stress you've been under lately. With Courtney and me out of your hair, you'll have more time to concentrate on your investigation."

"I like the two of you in my hair," Ross protested.

"And Jessica—" Ignoring Ross's comment, Fiona turned to their guest. "You have work of your own to finish. You don't need a toddler underfoot."

"Courtney's no problem," Jessica insisted with such fervor, Ross decided she wasn't simply being polite.

"Besides," Fiona continued, "with some unknown troublemaker stalking our family, Courtney and I both will be safer away from here."

"Safer!" The word erupted before Ross could rein in his impatience. "How can the two of you be safer, an elderly woman and a toddler, alone in Orlando?"

"We won't be alone," Fiona said with a smile that on anyone else Ross would have called smug.

"Who's going with you?" he demanded.

"No one," Fiona said. "Max Rinehart is meeting us there."

"Max?" Ross and Jessica asked in unison.

Fiona drank her coffee, totally composed in spite

of the bombshell she'd dropped. "Along with his oldest son, Fritz, and his wife and daughter, who happens to be the same age as Courtney."

"What child wouldn't want to go to Disney World?" Jessica said. "But Max? That's not his style."

"He only agreed," Fiona explained, "if Courtney and I promised to accompany him back to Miami for a week. Or two." She slid Ross a look from beneath half-closed eyelids, as if assessing his reaction.

Ross didn't know what to say. "I wanted to be the one to take Courtney to Walt Disney World."

"You'll have plenty of other opportunities," his grandmother assured him. "She'll appreciate a trip even more when she's older. But for now, don't you agree it's a good idea to have her out of the house? All these armed guards and strange goings-on can't be good for her."

Ross had to admit Fiona had a point, until a new thought struck him. "What if someone follows you to Orlando?"

"Has anyone from Swenson County been attacked away from home?" Fiona replied.

"No," Ross said, "not that I know of, but—"

"Then I see no problem." Fiona rose from the table and called to Chang Soo in the kitchen. "Bring my breakfast upstairs, please. I have to finish packing."

She breezed out of the room as quickly as she'd

entered, leaving Ross feeling as if he'd been hit by a late-spring twister.

"Well," he managed to utter to Jessica, "what do you think of that?"

"Your grandmother's a smart woman. Getting away will be good for Courtney. Even a child has to sense the tension around here."

There was tension, Ross thought, and then there was *tension*—the sexual kind, the kind he was feeling right now as he gazed at the woman across from him and wanted more than anything to pull her into his arms and taste her kisses again. But maybe keeping her here was selfish, letting his own needs overrule what was best for her.

"Would you like to join them?" he asked.

Her eyes widened in surprise. "Go to Disney World?"

"Sure. Why not? You could serve as a guide. You've been before, haven't you?"

An attractive shade of pale coral suffused her cheeks. "No, never."

"But Miami's not that far from Orlando," he said in amazement.

Jessica shifted in her chair as if the subject made her uncomfortable. "I spent most of my childhood in New England boarding schools and summer camps in the Adirondacks."

"And your parents never took you to Disney World?" he asked in disbelief.

"My parents were always on their honeymoon," she replied with a forlorn look.

"A perpetual honeymoon." The thought made his blood heat. "There could be worse things."

"There were. Their honeymoons weren't with each other. They've both been married several times."

A light went on in Ross's head. No wonder Jessica seemed so reluctant to relate to him. She'd never had an example of a loving couple to emulate. Ross, on the other hand, had witnessed the love and devotion of his parents, before their untimely deaths in a ski-slope avalanche, and of his grandparents. He knew that love between a man and woman could be one of life's greatest satisfactions.

Then why had he married Kathy, whom he didn't love? he asked himself.

The answer was obvious. Because at that time, he hadn't met Jessica Landon.

The pain of old memories shimmered in the deep blue of her eyes, and he wanted more than anything to chase away her hurt. "I've never been to Disney World, either," he assured her, neglecting to add that his grandparents had taken him to Disneyland several times.

"Boss—" Josh Greenlea, the deputy on duty at the house for the day shift, stepped into the dining room. "Carson Kingsley's at the front door. Says he wants to speak with you."

"Kingsley?" Ross asked in surprise. "Is there a problem at his ranch?"

Josh shrugged. "Couldn't get more than wanting to talk to you out of him."

"Send him in," Ross said.

The other night at the Chandlers' party had been the first time Ross had seen Carson out of the house—except for coming to town to buy supplies—since his wife died. His arrival this morning gave Ross a bad feeling deep in his gut. Something must have gone wrong at Longhorn Ranch. This visit surely couldn't be a social call.

When Carson entered the room, however, except for the usual sadness in his watery blue eyes and the stoop of his shoulders, too pronounced for a man not long past fifty, he appeared otherwise fine.

"Join us," Ross said, standing and indicating a chair. "You remember Miss Landon."

"Ma'am." Carson acknowledged Jessica with a nod and turned back to Ross. "Can't stay. Just wanted to bring this."

He held out a package, slightly bigger than a shoebox and wrapped in garish Christmas paper tied with a bright red bow.

Ross's suspicions kicked in. In all the years Carson had been their neighbor, he'd never come bearing gifts, not even at Christmas. The man must want something.

"It belonged to Susan," Carson explained, his voice breaking slightly on his dead wife's name.

"She loved it. And when I thought about little Courtney, spending another Christmas without her mother,
I wanted her to have it."

Remorse flooded Ross. So many bad things had
happened lately, wickedness was all he'd come to
expect. Evidently grief had mellowed his crusty
neighbor. The older man probably identified with
Courtney. Missing a loved one was especially hard
during the holidays. Ross always felt the loss of his
parents and grandfather more keenly during those
times.

He accepted the gift Carson offered. "That's
mighty thoughtful of you. Courtney will be pleased.
She loves presents. Sure you won't join us for breakfast?"

The rancher shook his head. "Had mine hours ago,
and I still have unfinished chores. Better get to 'em."

Without another word, he turned and left the room.

"What a nice thing to do," Jessica said.

"Too nice," Ross murmured, still perplexed by
his introverted neighbor's change of heart.

"What do you suppose it is?"

Ross picked up the package, hefted it and shook
it gently. "There's one way to find out." Without
hesitation, he slipped off the ribbon, then slit the tape
along the gift wrap with his table knife.

"But that's Courtney's present," Jessica protested.

"If it's something appropriate," Ross said, "I'll
rewrap it and let her have the pleasure of opening it.
If it's something she shouldn't have, I'll get rid of

it. Fiona will write Carson an appropriate note of thanks.''

He folded back the paper and lifted the lid off the box.

Jessica, who'd leaned forward for a better view, gasped. ''Oh, my gosh. It's wonderful.''

Ross looked from the contents to her. ''Guess you have to be female to appreciate it.''

''It's a collector's item,'' Jessica said. ''Worth hundreds of dollars.''

''It's just a doll,'' Ross said, ''but it's pretty and it looks brand new.''

''It's not just any doll,'' Jessica insisted. ''It's made by Madame Alexander. Her dolls are all historical or fictional characters. This one's Betsy Ross.''

Ross frowned. ''I'm sure Carson has no idea of its value. He's as tight with money as any man I ever met. I guess I should return it and explain.''

Jessica shook her head. ''He's made a generous gesture. You don't want to hurt his feelings.''

Ross sighed. ''You're right. I'll rewrap it and place it under the tree. Courtney can open it when she gets back from Florida.''

''You're okay with her going?''

Ross nodded. ''Fiona's right. Courtney shouldn't be exposed to the troubles here. Disney World will be a nice break.''

''Max and his son will keep a good eye on them,'' Jessica assured him.

"It was selfish of me to ask you to stay," Ross said, glad for the opportunity to make amends. "Maybe you should go with Fiona and Courtney. See Disney World for the first time."

She appeared confused. "You don't want me here?"

"This situation isn't easy on anyone."

Why was he saying that, when more than anything he wanted her to stay?

Because he cared what happened to her. Cared more than he wanted to admit.

He held his breath, waiting for her answer.

"I told you last night," Jessica said. "I'm secure enough here with the armed guards you've provided. And I'll be too busy straightening out the mess you call records—" she smiled as if to ease the harshness of her words "—to pay attention to much else."

Conflicting emotions pulled at him. He wanted her close, but even more he wanted her safe. He hoped the first would ensure the latter. "Max is lucky to have you."

The urge to tug her into his arms swept through him again. He fought against the distraction. If he was going to protect her, he had work to do.

"I'll talk to you later." He stood and headed toward the door.

"Ross—"

He stopped and turned toward her. "Yes?"

"About those gardenias…"

"Gardenias?" His mind was a blank. Then he remembered their earlier conversation, something about bushes in the solarium, but he had to concentrate on his work. "Oh, yeah. Glad you like them," he answered offhandedly, his mind flying in a million directions.

Her expression changed, but he couldn't tell if she was disappointed or confused.

He tucked away in the corner of his mind a reminder to check with the florist about the availability of gardenias. First, however, he had to meet with his detectives to see if they'd come up with any clue as to who was trying to kill Jessica. And why.

JESSICA SURVEYED THE LEDGERS on the desktop with mixed feelings. On the one hand, she was gradually bringing order out of the chaos of Ross's Shooting Star accounts. On the other, the progress was tedious, and it might take until the first of the year to complete her task.

She would finish sooner if she worked evenings, but she hadn't been able to force herself to abandon what had become a comfortable evening routine. Late every afternoon for the past four days, ever since Fiona and Courtney had left for Florida, Ross had joined her in his office. As soon as he returned to the ranch after his day's work, he'd stoke the fire, pour them both a drink, and they'd settle in the chairs in front of the fireplace while he reported on the progress—or lack of—in the investigation.

Just like an old married couple.

The comparison jolted her, but she couldn't escape its validity. She'd never felt so comfortable with another person, male or female, in her life as she did with Ross. She could be herself with him, not having to worry about professional or social impressions, but just enjoying his company, like that of a good friend.

Except a good friend didn't send her senses tingling as he did.

But friendship was all they shared, she assured herself, or she'd have taken the next available flight home. Ross hadn't tried to kiss her again, and no more floral tributes from the mysterious secret Santa had appeared on her pillow after he'd admitted sending the gardenias.

As if conjured up by her thoughts, Ross stepped into the room. "Making progress?" he asked.

She made a face, half scowl, half grin, and closed the ledger she'd been working on. "Cleaning up this act is like trying to move a mountain with a spoon."

"Ah, but persistence pays off."

"If I live to be a hundred and fifty," she cracked, "I might finish."

"Having you around that long would be nice." His tone was casual, and she could see only his back as he laid wood on the fire, but his words gave her a thrill.

Until her common sense kicked in. If there was anywhere she didn't want to spend the next one hundred and fifty years, it was in the wilds of Montana.

The American Virgin Islands, however, she'd consider.

An image of Ross, clad only in swim trunks and running through the surf, his body tan and lean, the sun glinting off his hair, formed in her mind before she gave herself a swift mental kick. Her feelings were merely the result of cabin fever. As soon as she left Montana and went back to the warm, open spaces of South Beach, Ross McGarrett would be a pleasant but distant memory, and her life would return to normal.

"How about you?" She took the glass of wine he offered and sank into her usual seat by the fire. "Any progress in the investigation?"

His drink in hand, Ross folded his long legs and sat opposite her. "Developments, but I wouldn't call them progress."

"Another attack?"

"No, thank God."

His voice was weary, and fatigue deepened the lines at the corners of his eyes. She understood why the people of Swenson County had elected him twice to the office of sheriff. No one in the county could care more about the welfare of its citizens than Ross did. Not solving the rash of crimes that plagued the area weighed visibly on him.

He sipped his drink, then gazed at her with disappointment etching his face. "Looks as if Dixon Traxler's definitely not a suspect."

"How can you be sure?"

"We've traced his activities since his release from prison, talked with his parole officer, were even given access to his financial records—"

"To track potential payments to an accomplice?"

Ross nodded. "Everything on the guy comes up squeaky clean. And no one else connected to his arrest or conviction has reported any problems."

"Then the attacks on me—"

"Weren't about you." Ross gazed at her, eyes filled with guilt. "I should have sent you home."

"I'm a big girl. I make my own decisions."

"Either you have an enemy no one's aware of, or someone's trying to get at me through you."

"That's ridiculous," she insisted. "The day I came to town, only John Hayes knew I was associated with—"

She suddenly recalled her wait in the café while the Crime Scene Unit secured the bank.

"You've thought of someone?" he asked.

"It's probably nothing."

"Who?" he insisted.

Jessica racked her brain, trying to recall the name on the waitress's name badge. "Madge."

"At the café?"

She nodded.

"You think Madge is trying to kill you?" If his tone hadn't told her, his expression would have indicated how preposterous he found her suggestion.

"I told her you'd recommended the pies. She jumped to the conclusion that I was your friend."

"Madge has a heart of gold. She wouldn't hurt a fly."

"But she also has a big, brassy voice. Everyone in the place must have heard her."

"How many customers were there?"

Jessica tried to picture the restaurant, but she'd been too impatient for her meeting that day to pay close attention to her surroundings. "Maybe two or three."

"Do you remember what they looked like?"

"All men. Stetsons, boots, blue jeans, tanned and weathered faces."

Ross grimaced.

"I know," Jessica said with a sigh. "I've just described half the county."

"At least it's a lead. I can talk to Madge, see if she remembers—"

"Sheriff—" The tall, skinny deputy who'd been on house duty that day stuck his head in the door. "Fire and Rescue just rolled."

"What's up?" Ross asked.

"Fire. At Longhorn Ranch."

"Mr. Kingsley's place?" Jessica asked.

Ross nodded. "Go give them a hand," he ordered the deputy.

"What about guarding Miss Landon?" the deputy said.

Ross pushed to his feet. "She and I are right behind you."

Chapter Eleven

Ross parked his vehicle directly behind the engine closest to the fire, unbuckled his seat belt and turned to Jessica. He'd been hesitant to bring her along and expose her to any danger, but he'd had to consider the possibility that a fire so close to the Shooting Star could be a diversionary tactic, intended to draw the inhabitants away. He'd decided Jessica was safer with him.

Hell, this wasn't the outing he'd been anticipating. He'd hoped to dazzle her with intimate dining at one of Billings's best restaurants, then take in the newest chick flick at the multiplex. He disliked romantic movies, but for Jessica, he'd forgo his usual action-adventure favorite. For her, he'd put up with damn near anything to make the right impression, to show her that he cared. He'd even considered escorting her to the annual Swenson Christmas dance at the hotel, in spite of the fact that getting all gussied up in a suit and tie wasn't his idea of fun. The torment would be worth it for the chance to hold her in his arms as they danced.

He stole a glance at the woman beside him, her cheeks rosy from the cold, her hair dusted with snow, her blue eyes reflecting the dangerous flames filling the sky ahead. An unfamiliar feeling clutched his heart. She'd had that powerful effect on him the first moment he saw her, and with every passing encounter, her impact grew stronger. He'd been waiting all his life for Jessica to come along, and now that she had, he didn't have a spare minute to spend with her alone.

"Stay close to me," he ordered, his voice grim.

The flames had been visible from the main road, leaping high into the star-studded night sky. At first, Ross had feared the main house was engulfed, but, after driving closer, had realized the fire was in a small outbuilding.

Without protest, Jessica climbed from the car and joined him. Together, they stepped over hoses running from the pumper truck and approached a group of men watching the firefighters work to extinguish the blaze.

"What have you got, Hank?" Ross asked the volunteer fire chief.

"It's my toolshed," Carson Kingsley, standing next to Hank, said. "Went up like a Roman candle all of a sudden. I tried to put it out, but…" He shook his head sadly.

Ross noted the older man's singed eyebrows and the bandages a paramedic was applying to his hands.

"Arson?" Ross asked Hank.

The fire chief shrugged. "Won't know till we can get in and investigate. Carson stores gas there for his tractor and other equipment. Could be spontaneous combustion. All that fuel makes a hell of a blaze."

Ross glanced at Jessica beside him, her face glowing in the flames, her eyes filled with sympathy for Carson, then turned back to Hank. "Any danger of this spreading?"

Hank shook his head. "The wind's light, and we have it under control. It shouldn't—"

The chief's radio crackled to life. "We have a fire in town, Chief. Gerald Gibson's house."

The chief started to curse, then, noting Jessica, stifled his words. He hit the microphone button. "Roll the other engine and call Grange County for assistance. I'm on my way."

"I'll leave my second-in-command in charge here," the chief said to Ross. "You staying, too?"

Ross grasped Jessica by the elbow and pivoted her toward his car. "I'd better check it out."

On the road into town, Jessica turned to him. "Do you investigate every fire in the county?"

"Not always. Gerald Gibson is our county tax collector." He uttered a silent prayer of thanks that Courtney and Fiona were in Florida, out of harm's way.

"Do you think the fire at the tax collector's house

is connected to the other crimes against government officials?'' Jessica asked.

"Could be. I want to check it out.''

"What about Mr. Kingsley? Does he work for the government, too?''

Ross shook his head. ''If the fire at Carson's wasn't a coincidence, it could have been a diversion, meant to draw firefighters to the other end of the county, away from Gibson's.''

Jessica shivered visibly.

"You warm enough?'' He wanted to pull her close, to assure her he'd protect her, but the console between the seats prevented that. Instead, he reached across and caressed her cheek with the back of his hand. ''Sorry to bring you out in this weather. I know you hate the cold.''

"That's the irony,'' Jessica said, gazing up at the sky through the windshield. ''It's such a beautiful night, in spite of the freezing temperature. Most people are preparing to celebrate a holiday dedicated to peace on earth and goodwill toward men, but you're searching for someone—or several someones—who want to wreak destruction on their neighbors.''

"Tonight's fires could have other explanations,'' Ross said. ''The Christmas season with its strings of lights, indoor trees, candles and other decorations, is a prime time for firefighters.''

"Does Carson decorate his toolshed?''

"Touché,'' Ross responded.

He'd tried to assuage her worries, but Jessica was

too smart not to see the probabilities. If tonight's fires were the acts of criminals stalking government officials, Ross hoped they'd been careless and left clues. Their luck at evading detection couldn't last forever.

If the so-called "freedom fighters" had set fire to Gibson's house, their attacks were escalating. He had to catch them before someone else died. With that thought in mind, he keyed the mike on his radio. "Patch me through to Fire and Rescue."

In seconds, he was talking with the lieutenant already on-site at the Gibson fire.

"Anyone hurt there?" Ross asked.

"Negative," came the response. "The family escaped, but the house is a goner."

"Thanks." Ross felt both relief and dismay. The Gibsons were unharmed but had lost not only their home, but probably everything they owned.

"This isn't just a job with you, is it?" Jessica asked.

"Swenson County is big in area, but small in population. I've known everyone here all my life. They're like family." He could feel the tension in the set of his jaw. "You mess with my family, you mess with me."

They drove the rest of the way into town in silence, the cheerful notes of carols on the radio an ironic counterpoint to his dark thoughts.

By the time they reached the street where the Gibson house had stood, the fire was out, and the volunteers were cooling down the hot spots.

Ross and Jessica stood on the fringes with the rest of the crowd, watching the mop-up. Ross used the opportunity to scan the crowd and make note of who was present. He caught sight of a familiar figure, passing cups of coffee and sweet rolls to the fire-fighters.

"Madge," he called. "Come over here."

The waitress from the café shouldered her way through the crowd to reach them. "Want some coffee, Sheriff?"

"No, thanks, I—"

"Hey," Madge said, looking at Jessica. "I remember you. You were in the day of the bank robbery."

"That's right," Jessica said. "I waited in your café until the dust settled."

"That's what I want to talk to you about." Ross lowered his voice so only Madge and Jessica could hear. "Who else was in the café that day, when Miss Landon was there?"

Madge puffed out her cheeks and closed her eyes, as if trying to remember. Then she let out her breath and looked at him. "Lots of excitement that day."

Ross nodded. "I don't expect you to remember—"

"Who could forget?" Madge said. "Before Miss Landon came in, we all watched the robber make his getaway with Josh on his heels."

"We?" Ross asked.

"There were three customers," Madge said.

"Two of them regulars. Jack Randall and Carson Kingsley."

"And the third?" Ross prodded her.

"Some stranger, just passing through, I guess. Never saw him before. Haven't seen him since."

"Thanks, Madge. And thanks for helping out tonight. I know the guys appreciate it."

"And the gals," Madge said with a wink. "Women are working with Fire and Rescue now, too."

Ross tried to process objectively the information Madge had just provided, setting aside the fact that Jack Randall was Courtney's grandfather. Three men had heard Madge's booming voice announce that Jessica was a friend of Ross's. Jack Randall had expressed his dislike for Ross often enough. He blamed Ross for his daughter's out-of-wedlock pregnancy, swore Ross was out to cheat him in their boundary dispute, and had made no secret that he held Ross accountable for his daughter's death.

"What do you think?" Jessica asked. "Any of Madge's customers suspects?"

"Jack Randall has plenty of reasons to strike out at me," Ross admitted.

"And Carson?"

Ross shrugged. "Carson's a weird duck. Hasn't seemed quite right since his wife died. But homicidal? Your guess is as good as mine."

"What about the third man," Jessica said. "The stranger?"

"Could have been someone just passing through." Jessica nodded.

"Then again," Ross said, "he could have been there on purpose."

"An accomplice to the bank robbery?"

"Possibly. Or a thug hired to hurt you. Someone who followed you to Swenson and the bank, then ran you off the road."

"Hey," she raised her voice in alarm, then lowered it again after a glance at the nearby crowd. "I thought you'd ruled me out as the prime target."

"I couldn't find any evidence to link Traxler to any attacks on you. My gut, however, insists the man's a fraud."

Jessica smiled, and the sweetness of her expression filled him with desire. "I agree Dixon's religious conversion is a bunch of hooey, concocted to turn him some fast bucks, but I doubt he's a killer. Or even has the gumption to hire one."

Ross stamped his feet to warm them, venting his frustration at the same time. "We're back where we started. But I'll check out Jack and Carson. Both use that highway regularly, and both drive dark pickups. First thing I'll do is have a look at their vehicles."

"It can't be pleasant," Jessica said with obvious empathy, "having to investigate your neighbors."

"We've got trouble, Ross." The fire chief joined them. "Arson. We can't do a full investigation until tomorrow, but Gibson's house was torched on purpose. There're signs of an accelerant at the rear entrance. The Gibsons were lucky to get out alive.''

"Smoke detectors?" Ross asked.

"We found the remains of three," the chief said with a scowl. "The batteries had been removed from all of them."

"My God," Jessica muttered beside him.

"If it hadn't been for the family dog's barking," Hank continued, "none of them would have survived."

Anger surged in Ross. Rage at the inhumanity of whoever had set the fire and exasperation at his own inability to catch the culprit.

"I'll meet you here at first light," Ross said to Hank. "We'll see what we can find."

The chief nodded and returned to his crew.

"Meanwhile—" Ross turned to Jessica "—there's nothing else we can do here. I'm taking you home."

JESSICA STEPPED from the claw-footed antique bathtub, toweled off and slipped on her velour robe. A long soak in hot water had finally chased the physical chill from her bones, but she felt cold all over again when she recalled the cruelty of the arsonist who'd tried to kill an entire family tonight.

Her heart went out to the Gibsons—and to Ross. She'd noted his frustration, as if he felt personally responsible for what had happened. He'd as much as said so in the car on the way home, blaming himself for not catching the killer—or killers—who stalked Swenson County.

His inability certainly hadn't been from lack of trying. She'd never met a man so dedicated to his work, so genuinely interested in the people he served. If she was ever to fall in love, it would be with a man like Ross McGarrett.

She faced herself in the mirror as she brushed her hair and noted the soft gleam in her eye, the silly smile on her face. She had to get a grip. Her heart was her own and no one else's. She had kept that vow all her life, and she wasn't about to break it for a handsome lawman, no matter how appealing. Unlike her parents, she planned to keep her heart intact, her emotions untouched. Life was easier that way.

Lonelier, too, an inner voice added, but she shoved that thought aside.

With a nod of determination at her reflection, she stepped into the bedroom.

And stopped short.

A magnificent bouquet of stargazer lilies and lilies of the valley, tied with bows of midnight blue shot with silver, covered her pillow. Someone had entered her room while she was bathing and left them there.

Ross?

Her heartbeat quickened at the thought.

With a shaking hand, she lifted the card that accompanied them.

"Jessica. I'll take care of you. Your secret Santa."

The ambiguity of the message brought the chill

back to her bones. If the flowers were from Ross, the card would be reassuring. But when she recalled questioning him about the gardenias, she realized his response had been distracted and unclear. If he'd sent the gardenias, someone else had to have delivered them for him, because she'd been with Ross when they'd been left on her pillow.

I'll take care of you.

Considering all that had happened to her since her arrival in Montana, and in light of the arson at the Gibson home tonight, the words seemed ominous, threatening.

She had only one way to resolve the puzzle.

She snatched the flowers from the bed, stormed out of the room, and down the hall. Pounding on Ross's bedroom door with her fist, she gathered up her courage to confront him. When the door swung open, she thrust the flowers in his face.

"Did you send these?" she demanded.

His face registered confusion—and another emotion she chose to ignore. "Not me. Fiona always puts the fresh flowers in the guest rooms."

"Fiona's not here."

Grabbing her elbow with one hand, he tugged her inside and shut the door with the other. With heavy draperies shut against the cold, logs blazing in the fireplace and a large fur rug nestled between the two deep chairs in front of the hearth, the room's intimacy enfolded her in its embrace.

She realized instantly she'd made a tactical error.

Finding herself confused, off balance, and consumed by an overwhelming physical attraction for the man, clad only in sweatpants, before her, she fought to regain control.

''And if she was here, would Fiona also leave cryptic notes?'' She thrust the secret Santa missive at him and watched his forehead knot into a frown as he read.

''This isn't the first one,'' she added.

''How many others?''

''Two.'' She repeated the messages on the first two notes.

''Why didn't you tell me about these before?'' Anger suffused his skin.

''Because it was too embarrassing. I thought you were playing cutesy games with me, and I didn't know how to respond.''

''You're shivering,'' he said.

Too late, Jessica realized she was dressed only in her robe—with nothing beneath it. And that her trembling was due to more than the chill. Ross's presence, tall, masculine, stimulating—and amazingly endearing—shook her to her core.

''Sit,'' he ordered.

Unable to resist, she allowed him to guide her to a chair by the fire. When she sat, he grabbed a blanket from his bed and tucked it over her lap with disarming gentleness. He pulled his own chair closer to hers and sank into it.

''Gardenias.'' He leaned toward her, his big hands

clasped between his knees. "Someone left gardenias on your pillow, too?"

Jessica nodded. "And before that a red rose."

"At least now that peculiar breakfast conversation about gardenias makes sense." He smiled, and his magnificent dark eyes widened with a sudden realization. "You thought I sent them?"

Jessica couldn't stop the flush that flooded her neck and face. "I figured it had to be you, Fiona or Chang Soo. Who else has access to the house?"

"Fiona's in Florida, so that rules her out." He shook his head in disbelief. "And Chang Soo? Even if he wanted to flatter you with his attention—and Chang Soo has never been much interested in the ladies—he wouldn't consider such an oblique approach honorable."

Ross rose suddenly, strode to his telephone and hit the button for the intercom to Chang Soo's room. While Jessica listened, he explained to the chef about the mysterious offerings that had appeared on Jessica's pillow.

Then he paused, listening.

"Chang Soo," he explained when he returned to his chair, "swears on the graves of his ancestors that he is not your secret Santa."

"And you believe him?"

"He's been with this family longer than I have. His loyalty and honesty are unquestionable."

She shivered again, in spite of the blanket. "So

someone else has been in the house. What if he's still here?''

Ross stood again, grabbed the radio off his bedside table and keyed the mike. ''Greenlea, I want a complete search of the house and grounds. Report to me when you're finished.''

''Ten-four, Sheriff,'' the reply came from the deputy, who was on duty at the house that evening.

Ross replaced the mike, removed his gun from the holster on the nightstand and sat next to her again.

''What now?'' she asked.

''We wait.''

Sitting with Ross so close in the intimacy of his bedroom took her thoughts and desires in dangerous directions. She tossed the blanket aside. ''I'll wait in my room.''

''No.''

He hadn't raised his voice, but simply placed the power of his authority and personality into that one simple word. It skewered her to her chair, even though her brain was telling her to get up and move or she was asking—begging—for trouble.

She didn't know how long they sat silently before the fire, listening to the logs crumble, observing the shower of sparks their deterioration created. All she knew was that her own breathing grew faster, her heartbeat quickened, and she wanted to be held, touched, loved by Ross in a way no other man had ever moved her.

Her tension grew so unbearable that she'd almost

convinced herself to bolt for the door, when Ross's radio sounded.

"The house and grounds are clear," Josh's voice announced. "Buck Bender and a couple of the hands helped me check. Everything's secure. And the house is locked up tight."

"Ten-four. And thanks." Ross replaced his gun in its holster.

Jessica pushed to her feet. "I can go back to my room now."

"No."

The word sounded again, but his tone this time was different, caressing rather than commanding. It set her skin tingling, her pulse pounding with anticipation.

He pulled her into his arms, placed a finger beneath her chin and tipped her face toward his. "Stay with me."

"But—"

"Or tell me you don't want to."

She opened her mouth to speak, but the lie wouldn't come. More than anything she'd ever wanted in her life, she wanted to spend this night with Ross.

The sexual release would be good for her, she reasoned, after all the tension she'd experienced. It was the twenty-first century, after all. She didn't have to love a man to enjoy the pleasures he could offer. She didn't have to make a commitment. But she had to be honest.

"There's something you should know," she said.

He raised an eyebrow, his expression curious. "What?"

"I don't get emotionally involved."

"Is that a *no*?"

"Emotional involvement isn't necessary for physical enjoyment." She silently cursed the catch in her breath.

"Not necessary, but definitely a plus," he countered.

"I don't want you jumping to conclusions."

A slow grin lit his face, already awash with firelight. "So you'll stay?"

Her brain, bombarded into chaos by the heat of his hard body pressed against hers, the delectable scent of him, the passion shining in his eyes, and the sound of his breathing, as tortured as her own, shut down. She was operating solely on desire. And pure, unadulterated pleasure.

She fumbled for words. "Just don't expect commitment. Along with sex."

"I'll consider myself duly warned." His expression was unreadable.

With a flick of his long fingers, he untied her sash, and her robe fell open, revealing her naked body.

His expression softened. "You're even more beautiful than I imagined."

His lips claimed her, and her mouth opened to him, their tongues entwining. He slid the robe from her shoulders and drew her down with him onto the fur rug before the hearth. In spite of her nakedness in the cool air, she felt as if her skin were aflame, the fire fanned by his touch, driving her to a frenzy of desire she'd never experienced before.

And then he was gone.

Dazed, biting her lip to keep from crying out in disappointment, she heard him enter the bathroom, open and close a drawer. In an instant, he was back, tossing a tiny, foil-wrapped package onto the rug beside them.

He slipped off his sweatpants, and she could see without doubt that his need was as great as hers. Lying beside her, he pulled her along the length of his bare body, and she shivered with delight at the delicious sensation of skin against skin and the captivating warmth of his body.

He nibbled kisses along her neck, over her breasts and down the curve of her stomach until she thought she would die with delight. His fingers found erotic spots she hadn't known existed, and she twined her own fingers in his hair, ran her nails lightly down his back, felt immense satisfaction at his swift intake of breath.

Positioning himself above her, he gazed into her eyes, a question posed in his own. "Tell me if you want me to stop."

"No."

"Even if I'm emotionally involved?" he asked. "Even if I'm committed?"

''No!'' The word burst from her lips as a plea, and she opened her arms and body to him.

He slid inside her as if they'd been made for each other alone, and the rhythm of his thrusts matched the beat of her heart. His gaze locked with hers, his eyes filled with feelings she couldn't avoid, couldn't deny. And she saw her own emotions reflected in them.

With fierce tenderness and a strange savage gentleness, he brought her to the brink of ecstasy. Together, they tumbled over the edge.

When he had regained his breath, he propped himself on one elbow and cupped her face with his other hand.

''I love you, Jessica. With all my heart.''

''I love you, too.''

The words sprang to her lips without thought of their consequences, and she couldn't call them back.

Chapter Twelve

The next morning before anyone else was awake,
Jessica dressed hurriedly and slipped from her room.
She left her luggage, packed and ready to be shipped.
Carrying anything other than the large handbag she
used for traveling would attract undue attention if she
ran into someone.

She'd been such a fool.

She'd had sex before, had enjoyed it before. But
she'd never made love. How could she have allowed
herself to fall in love with Ross McGarrett? And after
all the warnings she'd given herself, all her decla-
rations of intent to have her heart remain untouched
by the man?

Ross had fallen asleep beside her before the fire,
and as soon as his breathing had indicated deep sleep,
she'd covered him with a blanket, returned to her
room and packed.

After last night's shattering experience, she had
only one recourse if she wanted to keep her life on
an even keel. She was going back to Miami.

Today.

She'd hesitated briefly at the thought of setting out on her own, leaving the security of the guarded ranch. But if the secret Santa had been able to leave flowers three times on her pillow undetected, just how safe had she really been? She'd take her chances with a couple hours on the open road, locked in the security of her vehicle, in order to return to Miami, away from SCOFFS and secret Santas.

And Ross.

In the silent kitchen, where even the early-rising Chang Soo hadn't yet appeared, she reached for the set of keys to Fiona's car. They hung with others on a board beside the door. Jessica would leave the car in long-term parking at the airport, and Fiona could claim it on her return from Miami.

"You all right?"

She almost jumped out of her skin at the sound of Josh Greenlea's voice. The deputy had been on duty all night, and the last thing she wanted was for him to alert Ross before she could get away.

"I have an early meeting at the bank," she lied.

"Ross know you're going into town without an escort?" Josh looked skeptical.

"He asked me to take one of the hands with me," Jessica lied again. "I'll pick him up at the bunkhouse."

Josh nodded and started to brew coffee. Jessica made her escape.

The snow crunched beneath her feet, the noise so

loud she was certain it would awaken Ross, still asleep in his room on the second floor. But no light appeared in the window even at the rumble of the garage door's opening.

For an instant, she hesitated, reluctant to leave, remembering the warmth and contentment of Ross's embrace, the electrifying passion of their lovemaking. There were worse things in the world than loving a man.

Like having that love disappear, leaving your world in ruins, your heart in pieces.

She hardened her resolve, unlocked the car and tossed her bag inside.

With a sigh of relief that no one had tried to stop her, Jessica slid behind the wheel, started the car and eased down the driveway toward the main road.

By the time she reached the highway, dawn was lightening the eastern sky. She pressed the accelerator, and the car responded with a burst of speed.

Soon she'd be on a plane headed home, and Ross and last night's lovemaking would be only a memory.

One she could never forget.

With a mixture of determination and regret, she continued her journey.

Until the car sputtered and died.

ROSS AWAKENED, remembering instantly how complete he'd felt last night with Jessica in his arms. He reached for her beside him and found only thin air.

Ashes filled the fireplace, and, without the blaze, the room had cooled. With a groan, he rolled over and eyed the clock beside his bed: 10:30 a.m.

He'd overslept. Big-time. Not that he hadn't needed the rest. He'd put in a hell of a week. And loving Jessica last night had somehow drained all the stress from him, giving him the best rest he'd had in days. He stretched, ready to roll into the blanket and sleep again, when he recalled his scheduled meeting with the fire chief and the arson investigators. He was already a couple hours late.

After a quick shower, he dressed and hurried downstairs, hoping Jessica was awake and at work in his office so he could see her before he left. The kitchen was empty of people but filled with the tantalizing aroma of Chang Soo's coffee. Ross was pouring himself a cup to take with him when the chef entered the kitchen, his ancient face contorted in a frown.

"Something wrong?" Ross asked.

Chang Soo handed him a bundle of letters. "Buck brought the mail from the box by the gate. That first envelope was on top."

Ross glanced at the papers the chef had given him. The first envelope was a standard size, but instead of a written or typed address, the letters R-O-S-S had been cut from a magazine or newspaper and pasted on.

"What the hell?" Grabbing a paper towel, Ross lifted the strange missive gingerly and held it to the light. Only the shadow of a single sheet of folded paper was visible. Chang Soo passed Ross a paring knife, and Ross carefully slit the envelope. Using the paper towel in hopes of preserving any fingerprints, he withdrew the folded sheet and opened it.

The message, in the same cut letters, made his blood run cold.

WE HAVE JESSICA LANDON. YOU WON'T SEE HER ALIVE AGAIN.

SCOFF.

Ross's world reeled. The message had to be a prank. Jessica was here at the ranch, secure under the watchful eye of his deputy and ranch hands.

"Have you seen Jessica this morning?" Ross asked the chef.

Chang Soo shook his head. "She hasn't been downstairs yet."

On the desperate hope that the strange message was an idle threat, Ross took the stairs to the second floor two at a time and threw open the door to the guest room. Jessica's luggage sat on the bed. The closet was empty, and her makeup and toiletries had been removed from the bathroom.

Ignoring the anguish that crushed his heart, he picked up the phone beside the bed. Josh Greenlea had gone off duty at eight. He'd be home by now, ready for bed after working all night.

"Did you see Miss Landon this morning?" Ross

demanded before Josh even had a chance to say hello.

"Sure," the deputy replied. "In the kitchen around six-thirty. She was taking Mrs. McGarrett's car into town for a meeting at the bank."

"And you let her go alone?"

"She said you'd arranged for one of the hands to go with her. She was picking him up at the bunk-house."

Ross took a deep breath and struggled for control. Reaming out Josh wouldn't help in finding Jessica. He explained to Josh about the note, asked the deputy to return to the ranch and hung up.

Downstairs, he called the dispatcher, asked her to cancel his meeting with the fire chief and ordered her to put out an immediate all-points bulletin for Fiona's car. Then he had Chang Soo call the bunkhouse to see if anyone actually had accompanied Jessica.

Chang Soo quickly reported that all hands were accounted for.

A few minutes later, Josh Greenlea called in on the radio. "I'm on my way to the ranch, and I found Mrs. McGarrett's car."

"Where?"

"On the side of the road, just a few miles outside of town."

"Any signs of what happened?"

"Miss Landon's purse is on the front seat. Money's still in her wallet. Credit cards, too. And the fuel gauge is on empty."

Ross stifled a curse. He never had been able to get his grandmother to keep her car gassed and ready, even though the pump was right there at the garage. Whenever Fiona started out anywhere, Ross, Chang Soo or Buck had to remind her to fill up her tank. Jessica had probably borrowed Fiona's car and not bothered to check the gauge. When she ran out of gas, someone had probably offered her a lift to a gas station and abducted her instead.

Ross's thoughts flew in every direction, returning always to the question of why Jessica had left without saying where she was going. Or goodbye.

Their lovemaking last night had been satisfying, exciting, the best sex he'd ever had—because he'd had it with a woman he loved. He'd thought Jessica had felt the same. She'd even said she loved him. So why had she fled the Shooting Star at first light?

Focus, dammit, he swore at himself. He'd never find Jessica alive if he didn't concentrate on the facts and keep his feeling under wraps.

What if she's already dead?

He refused to consider that possibility.

So what did he have to go on? After picking her up on the highway, her abductor could have headed north through town. No, Ross shook his head, talking to himself. That wasn't right. The kidnapper had had to travel south to leave the message in the mailbox by the gate.

Ross keyed his radio mike and spoke to the dispatcher. ''Check with the post office. Find out who's making deliveries on our rural route today. Have a deputy track down the letter carrier and ask who he's seen on the road between here and town this morning.''

''Yes, sir. We're on it.''

Ross took the coffee Chang Soo handed him, sat at the table and studied the note. Whoever had composed it had to live nearby. Unless the abductor had known in advance that Jessica would be stranded on the highway so he could be ready to grab her, he'd had to return someplace to put together the letter he'd then left for Ross. And he hadn't had time to travel any great distance.

Jack Randall and Carson Kingsley came to mind. Both were neighbors. Both had been in the café the day of the bank robbery and were potential suspects in the attack on Jessica's rental car.

Or both his neighbors could be completely innocent, and Jessica the victim of a killer hired by Dixon Traxler, one who'd cleverly tried to pin the blame for her disappearance on the local pain-in-the-ass militia group.

There was only one way to find out. Ross didn't like the task that faced him, but with Jessica's life on the line, he had no choice.

TWENTY MINUTES LATER, having driven to town at speeds over ninety miles an hour with lights blazing and sirens wailing, Ross entered the interrogation room of the county jail. Miles Garrigan, the man who had robbed the bank the day of Jessica's arrival in Swenson, sat at a table.

Dressed in faded blue prison-issue clothes and slippers, minus his Santa beard, suit and padding, the man seemed shriveled, smaller than Ross remembered. And several days in jail had sapped his cocky attitude. This time Miles greeted Ross, not with his usual sneer, but with an apprehensive look.

Not liking what he had to do, but determined to follow through, Ross removed his gun, his watch, his ring. He handed them to the deputy on duty and dismissed him.

"You hear anything coming from this room, ignore it," Ross said, "unless it's my voice calling your name."

The deputy nodded grimly, left and locked the door behind him.

Ross strode to the table, flattened both hands on its surface and leaned until his face was inches from the robber's.

"We can do this easy," Ross said with a scowl, "or we can do it the hard way."

Garrigan squirmed in his chair. "What are you talking about?"

"SCOFF," Ross said.

Garrigan's eyes flicked to the side, refusing to meet Ross's glance. "Don't know what you're talking about."

Unwilling to reveal his regret at the man's answer, Ross deepened his scowl. He'd never hurt a prisoner, didn't believe in strong-arm tactics. But Garrigan didn't know that. Ross intended to scare him within an inch of his life to make him give up what he knew. Right now Garrigan was his best hope of finding Jessica fast.

Crime techs were dusting the car and note for prints and checking the paper and envelope for possible suppliers, but following those leads could take days. Ross wanted to find Jessica. Now.

He grabbed the prisoner by the front of his shirt and practically lifted him from his chair. "My gut tells me you know all about SCOFF, and my gut's never wrong."

Garrigan's face was turning red from lack of air due to Ross's twist on the man's collar. But he said nothing.

"You're already in a heap of trouble," Ross said, dropping the prisoner suddenly back into his seat. "Guess you're not worried about murder. Or the death penalty."

"Murder?" Garrigan licked his dry lips and rubbed his neck where his collar had choked him.

"SCOFF's already killed once. And they're prepared to kill again."

"Don't even know what SCOFF is," Garrigan insisted, but not very convincingly.

"Guess you're not concerned about your family, either," Ross said.

"What about my family?"

"The sheriff of Grange County's a friend of mine.

Wouldn't take but a nod from me for him and his deputies to make your family miserable," Ross lied. "Parking tickets here, moving violations, tickets for disobeying zoning regulations. Maybe even arresting your teenage son as a juvenile offender—"

"Wait," Garrigan cried, "you can't do that. My wife's upset enough already—"

"You think I give a damn?" Ross shouted in the man's face, lying again, turning up the pressure. "Someone in SCOFF has abducted the woman I love and threatened to kill her. I should be concerned about your wife?"

Garrigan shrank in his chair.

"In fact," Ross continued with his charade of abuse, "nothing would give me greater satisfaction than to beat the crap out of you now *and* make your family miserable for the rest of their days."

"You can't do that." Garrigan seemed to regain a fraction of his courage. "It's against the law."

"In this county, I am the law." Ross drew back his fist as if ready to strike. "Now what's it going to be? Answer my questions or get the beating of your life?"

"Stop!" Garrigan threw his arms in front of his face, indicating what Ross had instinctively known. The man was all bravado, a coward at heart. He'd probably sell out his best friend to save his own skin.

"I'll tell you whatever you want to know," the prisoner whined.

"That's better." Ross dropped his arm. He yanked

out the chair across the table from Garrigan, turned it backward and straddled it. "Now, we'll start with SCOFF. Who's in it and where can I find them?"

JESSICA STRAINED against the ropes that tied her to the straight-backed chair, then stopped in frustration. Her movements only drew the bonds tighter. She had to face reality. There was nothing she could do. Unless someone showed up to rescue her, she was at her captor's mercy.

And he'd already promised to kill her.

Carson Kingsley sat in his easy chair in front of the fire, sipping whiskey and ignoring the sandwich he'd fixed himself for lunch. He hadn't offered her anything. Not even a glass of water for her parched lips.

She prayed for Ross to come, but she didn't have much hope. He wouldn't have a clue where she was. No one would suspect Kingsley, especially after his generous gift of the Madame Alexander doll to Courtney. After all, he was merely a grieving and eccentric widower to most people, nothing like the agitated man with a maniacal gleam in his eye who was planning to kill her.

He'd seemed harmless enough when he'd stopped his battered station wagon beside Fiona's car on the highway.

"Need a lift?" he'd asked.

Jessica had been overcome with relief at his appearance. She was anxious to make her escape before Ross passed her on the road on his way to work.

"Out of gas," she replied.

"Station in town's not open yet," Kingsley said.

"I don't want to go back to the Shooting Star." If she returned, she'd succumb to the emotion welling in her now, an incredible desire to throw herself into Ross's arms and never let go, never leave.

"I've got gas at my place," Kingsley said. "We can run back there and pick it up. Have you on the road in no time."

"You're a good neighbor," Jessica said.

"Try to be," he'd said with a smile and gallantly opened the passenger door for her.

Everything had seemed fine until he pulled into the barn next to a large black pickup truck. Its right side was battered and scraped and bore traces of paint the same color as that of the car Jessica had rented. His gaze followed hers.

"Damn," he muttered. "Wish you hadn't seen that."

Sudden realization grabbed her by the throat, squeezed the breath from her lungs. "You're the one who ran me off the road. But I'm sure it was an accident," she added quickly and with a nonchalance she didn't feel.

"Had to teach Ross McGarrett a lesson," Kingsley muttered. "Thought he'd get out of government after his wife died. He'd be a good man if he stuck with ranching. It's them government types. Can't trust 'em. Bleed you dry.''

The man's crazy ramblings accelerated her fear. She tried to stay calm.

''I'm not that far from the Shooting Star.'' She tried to keep her voice reasonable and steady and grabbed the door handle. ''I can walk back from here. Thanks for the lift.''

''Stay where you are.'' Kingsley reached beneath the seat, pulled out a revolver and aimed it at her. ''And do what I tell you.''

He'd brought her into the house, tied her up and then sat at a table with paper, scissors, an old copy of *Time* and a bottle of glue. After constructing some kind of note and sealing it in an envelope, he left.

While he was gone, Jessica had too much time to think. And all she could think of was Ross. His courage, his dedication to duty, his slow, sexy smile, the excitement of his touch. The more she thought, the more she realized there were worse things than loving and losing someone. The very worst was never having the chance to love at all. Her eyes misted with tears. At least he'd know how she'd felt about him. Earlier she'd regretted admitting last night that she loved him. Now she was glad she'd said the words aloud.

Kingsley had returned, too quickly to have made a trip into town, and Jessica could only surmise that he'd left the note he'd constructed from magazine letters at the Shooting Star. But even though the man seemed crazy, he was too wily to have let Ross know who he was, where he was. After all, Kingsley had managed to elude the entire Swenson County Sheriff's Department for over a year.

While Carson muttered into his drink, Jessica studied the room, hoping to find a means of escape. Every surface was stacked with pamphlets and flyers, all antigovernment propaganda from various militia groups, judging from the ones closest that she could read. Her abductor obviously hated anyone and everyone connected with government.

"Did you start the fire at the Gibsons' last night?" she asked.

Carson nodded glumly. "Botched that job. And set my own shed afire by accident when I came home and was putting away my tools and gas can."

"The house is a total loss."

"Did they all die?" His eyes lighted in anticipation.

Jessica shook her head. "The dog warned them. The whole family got out in time."

"Thought about the dog. Considered killing it, but couldn't do it. I love animals."

Jessica closed her eyes. Carson Kingsley was clearly out of his mind. After what he'd done to Kathy McGarrett and the Gibson family, he wouldn't hesitate to kill her, too. Her only hope was to keep him talking, keep him from acting until someone figured out where she was—or stumbled onto her by accident.

Her gaze lit on an object on the mantel. A Lladró figurine of a young woman with a flock of geese at her feet. "You broke into Judge Chandler's house."

"Yep." Carson sipped his drink. "Harry's part of the government, too."

"But Julie isn't. Why torment her?"

"To teach Harry a lesson. I could have killed her, but the time wasn't right yet."

"Right?"

"What's the good of just killing somebody if they don't suffer first? You just put 'em out of their misery."

"Did you steal the judge's rifle?"

Carson looked smug. "The night of the party. Everybody was so blamed busy socializing, I just waltzed it out practically under their noses."

"Why?"

"To throw Ross off the track. The man's too smart. Had to make him think that smart-mouthed author might have been the shooter." He laughed softly to himself. "Yes, Ross has to suffer. They all have to suffer."

Jessica swallowed hard against the nausea rising in her throat, wondering if Carson intended to torture her before he killed her. She wiggled her feet and hands to drive away the numbness from restricted blood flow and tried to keep him talking.

"You're the secret Santa, aren't you?"

He looked at her as if she were the crazy one. "I don't know what the hell you're talking about."

"The notes. The flowers."

He shook his head. "I don't hold with such foolishness."

Jessica's mind whirled. If Carson hadn't put the flowers and messages on her pillow, who had? If she didn't keep him talking, she wouldn't live long enough to find out.

"Did you shoot at me that morning in the solarium?"

"Naw, not *at* you. I'm a good shot. Could have killed you or Ross that morning if I'd wanted to."

"But why me? I'm not connected to the government."

"Because hurting you hurts Ross. I heard Madge at the café say you're a friend of his. And I saw how he looked at you that night at Chandlers' party. Like a man with his heart in his eyes. Same as at breakfast the other day when I brought the doll. The man loves you. It's written all over his face."

Jessica remembered Ross's expression when they'd made love the night before. More than anything in the world, she wanted to see that look one more time before she died.

Keep talking.

"Why bring his daughter a doll if you hate Ross so much?"

Carson's face softened with a smile. "Susan loved children. We could never have them. That's why she started that doll collection. They were her babies."

"You miss her, don't you?"

"Shut up!" Carson pushed out of his chair and grabbed his gun from a nearby table. "It's time Ross McGarrett experiences again what it's like to lose someone he loves."

Jessica closed her eyes. The end was coming. She thought fleetingly of Max and Miami, but her heart was centered on Ross, the man she'd never have a chance to love.

At Carson's gasp of surprise and an unexpected burst of cold air, she opened her eyes.

Ross stood in the doorway, gun drawn, his face tight with anger.

"Put the gun down, Carson."

Carson didn't lower his weapon.

"You all right, Jessica?" Ross spoke to her but kept his sights fixed on Kingsley.

"I am now." She didn't know how he'd found her, but it didn't matter. Everything was going to be fine with Ross in control.

"Glad you're here, Ross," Carson said with a maniacal cackle. "Now I can kill you both."

"You don't want to do that," Ross said quickly. "The place is surrounded by a SWAT team. One move other than to drop your weapon and a sharpshooter will drill you right between the eyes."

"You're lying."

"I don't lie."

Carson's gaze flicked to the window. Jessica followed his glance. A black-clad rifleman stood out starkly against the snow-covered field, the sun glinting off the glass of his scope.

The older man must have retained some vestige of sanity, or at least hadn't developed a death wish. Slowly, carefully, he laid his gun on the table and raised his hands.

Then all hell broke loose.

The SWAT team, their faces covered by black ski masks, their bodies armored with helmets and bulletproof vests, burst into the room from the kitchen and through the door behind Ross. In seconds, they had Carson handcuffed, had read him his rights and cut Jessica's bonds.

The instant she was free, she leaped into Ross's arms and kissed him with all the pent-up longing for the lifetime she'd feared she would never have. He held her fast, as if he never wanted to release her, and returned her kiss with a fervor that left her weak.

After a moment, he drew back, his eyes shining, his endearing grin wreathing his face.

"That was some kiss," he teased. "Good thing you don't get emotionally involved. The impact might have killed me."

She returned his smile, her heart soaring. "You want emotional involvement? I'll show you emotional involvement."

She kissed him again, so wrapped in his love she barely noticed the cheers and applause of the surrounding SWAT team.

Epilogue

"For someone who hates Christmas," Ross said softly, somehow managing to nibble her ear at the same time, "you seem amazingly content."

Jessica snuggled closer, cuddling against him on the sofa in front of the blazing fire. The only other illumination in the room came from the tiny white lights twinkling on the nine-foot decorated tree in the corner beside the hearth.

"I never knew what Christmas was really like before," she admitted. "Yours was the first tree I ever helped decorate. Not to mention the first I ever went into the woods to find and help cut."

"That was some sleigh ride," Ross recalled with a grin.

Jessica blushed at the memory. Naked beneath the furs and blankets, they'd made love in the sleigh. If it hadn't been for the heat of their passion, they'd have suffered serious frostbite.

"A regular part of your Christmas tradition?" she asked with a sidelong glance.

"I plan to make it that way," he admitted.

"Then you'll have to make sure Fiona and Courtney go to Miami at tree-cutting time each year."

"Speaking of Courtney," Ross said, "it's almost time for Santa to make his appearance."

"You're sure she's asleep?" Jessica asked.

"Probably not, but I warned her if she interrupted Santa, he wouldn't leave her anything."

Jessica stared at the fire, feeling safe and snug in Ross's arms. Recalling her brush with death at Carson Kingsley's hands, she shivered.

"What's wrong?" Ross asked.

"Just thinking about Carson."

"You don't have to worry about him. He's locked up for a long time. And undergoing psychiatric evaluation."

"Was he always crazy?"

Ross shrugged. "Maybe. Either Susan kept him under control or else her death pushed him over the edge. His paranoia about government is totally irrational."

"What's going to happen to the bank robber?" Jessica asked.

"I've put in a good word about his cooperation in helping me find you."

"And he was part of SCOFF?"

"Carson had recruited him," Ross explained. "The purpose of the robbery was to fill SCOFF's coffers with funds to wage their antigovernment war."

"Are there other members?"

"When Garrigan realized he might gain a lighter sentence, he told us the names of everyone who'd ever expressed the slightest interest in their cause. Before the end of the month, we'll have the whole rotten bunch rounded up."

"The end of the month," Jessica murmured. "My report will be finished by then."

"Will I pass muster?" Ross asked, looking amused.

"Not financially," Jessica said with a grimace. "If you didn't spend so much time as sheriff, you could make the Shooting Star twice as profitable. I don't know what Fiona's reaction to that fact will be."

"You think she'll refuse to transfer the ranch to my name?" Ross said.

"She's your grandmother. You know her better than I."

"There was never any question about the ranch coming to me." Ross shook his head in admiration. "She's a schemer."

"The secret Santa bit?" Jessica asked.

"It goes deeper than that," Ross said. "She confessed everything to me. First she and Max Rinehart conspired to throw you and me together. Then Fiona enlisted Chang Soo as her deliveryman, hoping you'd think the secret Santa flowers and messages were from me. It's a wonder she didn't just steal our clothes and lock us naked in a room together." He appeared thoughtful. "That would have worked."

Jessica slapped him playfully on the upper arm. "You are so bad."

"Want to see how bad I can be?" he asked with a suggestive leer.

"What if Santa shows up?" she asked. "We wouldn't want him to catch us being naughty."

"That reminds me." Ross released her, stood and went to the tree. After burrowing in the pile of gifts beneath it, he returned to her with a small box in his hand. "This is for you. From your not-so-secret Santa."

He placed the black velvet box in her hand. "Open it."

Her heart beating with excitement, Jessica lifted the lid. Myriad diamonds winked at her, set in a yellow-gold band. The largest was a star, and the smaller ones formed a meteor trail, just like the Shooting Star's brand.

Her breath caught in her throat. "It's beautiful."

"It's the Shooting Star. I'm offering it to you."

Her eyes widened in amazement. "You're giving me your ranch?"

He took the ring and slid it onto the third finger of her left hand. "Half of it anyway. That's what marriage means. We share everything. Will you marry me, Jessica?"

His proposal left her speechless, and when she didn't respond, anxiety spread across his face. "We could spend some of the winter in Miami, since you hate the cold."

She still couldn't speak past the lump in her throat.

"Or all winter, if that's what it takes," he offered as if in desperation.

Suddenly she found her voice. "Oh, yes," she whispered.

"Winters in Miami?" he asked.

She admired the sparkle of the diamonds in the firelight before wrapping her arms around his neck and lifting her face to his.

"Winters *any*where," she said, "as long as we're together."

"Oh, I plan for us to be together for a long, long time. An eternity, at least."

"That might be long enough," she said, and kissed him.

* * * * *

Check out Charlotte Douglas's
December 2003 book, DR. WONDERFUL,
from Harlequin American Romance.

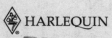

HARLEQUIN
INTRIGUE

COMING NEXT MONTH

#741 A WARRIOR'S MISSION by Rita Herron
Colorado Confidential
When Colorado Confidential agent Night Walker arrived to investigate the Langworthy baby kidnapping, he discovered that the baby was *his*. A night of passion with Holly Langworthy months ago had left him a father, and now it was up to him to find his son—and win the heart of the woman he'd never forgotten.

#742 THE THIRD TWIN by Dani Sinclair
Heartskeep
Alexis Ryder's life was turned upside down the day she came home to find her father murdered, a briefcase full of money and a note revealing she was illegally adopted. Desperate to learn the truth, she had no choice but to team up with charming police officer Wyatt Crossley—the only man who seemed to have the answers she was seeking.

#743 UNDER SURVEILLANCE by Gayle Wilson
Phoenix Brotherhood
Phoenix Brotherhood operative John Edmonds was given one last case to prove himself to the agency: keep an eye on Kelly Lockett, the beautiful heir to her family's charitable foundation. But their mutual attraction was threatening his job—and might put her life in danger....

#744 MOUNTAIN SHERIFF by B.J. Daniels
Cascades Concealed
Journalist Charity Jenkins had been pursuing sexy sheriff Mitch Tanner since they were children. Trouble was, the man was a confirmed bachelor. But when strange things started happening to Charity and Mitch realized she might be in danger, he knew he had to protect her. Would he also find love where he least expected it?

#745 BOYS IN BLUE by Rebecca York (Ruth Glick writing as Rebecca York), Ann Voss Peterson and Patricia Rosemoor
Bachelors At Large
Three brothers' lives were changed forever when one of their own was arrested for murder. Now they had to unite to prove his innocence and discover the real killer...but they never thought they'd find *love*, as well!

#746 FOR THE SAKE OF THEIR BABY by Alice Sharpe
When her uncle's dead body was found in his mansion, Liz Chase's husband, Alex, took the rap for what he thought was a deliberate murder by his pregnant wife. But once he was released from prison, and discovered that his loving wife hadn't committed the crime, could they work together to find the *real* killer... and rekindle their relationship?

Visit us at www.eHarlequin.com

HICNM1103

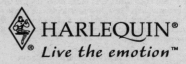

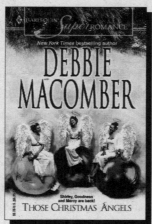

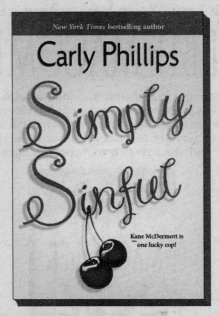
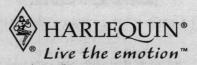

If you enjoyed what you just read,
then we've got an offer you can't resist!

Take 2 bestselling
love stories FREE!
Plus get a FREE surprise gift!

Clip this page and mail it to Harlequin Reader Service

IN U.S.A.	IN CANADA
3010 Walden Ave.	P.O. Box 609
P.O. Box 1867	Fort Erie, Ontario
Buffalo, N.Y. 14240-1867	L2A 5X3

YES! Please send me 2 free Harlequin Intrigue® novels and my free surprise gift. After receiving them, if I don't wish to receive anymore, I can return the shipping statement marked cancel. If I don't cancel, I will receive 6 brand-new novels each month, before they're available in stores! In the U.S.A., bill me at the bargain price of $3.99 plus 25¢ shipping and handling per book and applicable sales tax, if any*. In Canada, bill me at the bargain price of $4.74 plus 25¢ shipping and handling per book and applicable taxes**. That's the complete price and a savings of at least 10% off the cover prices—what a great deal! I understand that accepting the 2 free books and gift places me under no obligation ever to buy any books. I can always return a shipment and cancel at any time. Even if I never buy another book from Harlequin, the 2 free books and gift are mine to keep forever.

182 HDN DU9K
382 HDN DU9L

Name	(PLEASE PRINT)	
Address	Apt.#	
City	State/Prov.	Zip/Postal Code

* Terms and prices subject to change without notice. Sales tax applicable in N.Y.
** Canadian residents will be charged applicable provincial taxes and GST.
  All orders subject to approval. Offer limited to one per household and not valid to
  current Harlequin Intrigue® subscribers.
  ® are registered trademarks of Harlequin Enterprises Limited.

INT03

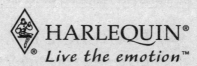

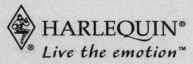